Praise

My Darling D

"A treasure . . . the book begs to be picked up. *My Darling Dead Ones* is all about memory; how a word, a gesture, can sweep you backwards in time. Reading it can seem like sifting through a box of family souvenirs. . . . de Vasconcelos has woven gold from straw. . . . Her writing is smooth and self-assured, a pleasure to read."
Halifax Daily News

"A gob-smacking novel . . . visually striking. . . . *My Darling Dead Ones* is written with the linguistic sensitivity of the exile. [It] is a remarkably unmorbid elegy for the dead by the living and a distinctively accomplished first novel. Tilling language in much the same way as her characters till the earth, de Vasconcelos has nurtured a most life-affirming narrative of death."
The New Brunswick Reader

"Emotionally engaging. . . . It's a book that distils authentic experience and peddles its feminism lightly. Women will enjoy it . . . and men, too."
The Toronto Star

"Erika de Vasconcelos has a lush and tantalizing way with a story: she foreshadows and backtracks, building up tension, then replaying events after the fact in the mind."
The Montreal Gazette

"Memories of Portugal . . . are rendered with supple, sensuous immediacy. The book's emphasis on memory and what we inherit from those we defy is reminiscent of Margaret Laurence. The forward-backward structure mirrors the journey Fiona takes into her family's past, as a way to come to terms with her present. The result is like an album of family photographs that catches us off guard by collapsing time, showing us something of ourselves in the images of the past."
The Calgary Herald

"[*My Darling Dead Ones*] has the intense and urgent cadence of a whispered confidence, and de Vasconcelos' flair for economical description is particularly potent in evoking the sights, sounds and smells of Portugal."
NOW Magazine

"What is especially wonderful about *My Darling Dead Ones* is the abundance of life teeming through its pages: the Portuguese landscape of hilly, yellow-stuccoed houses is palpable; Magdalena's flat in Lisbon invites exploration of its quaint clutter; one sniffs the scent of fresh earth as Leninha creates a back room of hostas and calla lilies in her suburban Montreal garden. [Here] is a complex and sumptuous world . . . there is much comfort, beauty and delight in *My Darling Dead Ones*."
Quill & Quire

"A compelling story of four strong, intelligent, passionate women. . . . de Vasconcelos' writing style is effective and purposeful. . . . A lovely, even beautiful novel."
The Sherbrooke Record

My Darling Dead Ones

a novel

Erika de Vasconcelos

VINTAGE CANADA
A Division of Random House of Canada

FIRST VINTAGE CANADA EDITION, 1998

Canadian Cataloguing in Publication Data

de Vasconcelos, Erika
My darling dead ones

ISBN 0-676-97151-2

I. Title.

PS8557.E8437M92   1998   C813'.54   C97-932414-9
PR9199.3.D48M92   1998

Printed and bound in the United States of America

10 9 8 7 6 5 4 3

For my parents
and
In memory of my three grandmothers

Helena de Sousa Fillol Machado
Magdalena Fillol
Maria Mercês Mendes de Vasconcelos

I say, Write.
She say, What?
I say, Write.
She say, Nothing but death can keep me from it.
                    Alice Walker, THE COLOR PURPLE

ACKNOWLEDGEMENTS

I gratefully acknowledge the financial support of the Toronto Arts Council, the Ontario Arts Council and the Explorations program of the Canada Council.

I would like to thank my agent, Janet Turnbull Irving, for her extraordinary enthusiasm and professionalism. For their wisdom, encouragement and support I would like to thank the following: Nino Ricci, Dorothy Bennie, Paul Quarrington, Martha Johnson, Mark Gane, Richard Lewis and Paula de Vasconcelos. I am indebted to Allison Maclean for her generous advice and recommendation of my work. I would also like to thank my editor, Louise Dennys, for the exactness of her insights; she understood the book more fully, at times, than even I did.

Special thanks to Stephanie Morgenstern, friend and mentor, for two decades of erotica, and for a fabulous letter, and to Thomas McKendy, my dearest teacher, for not giving the answers.

Most importantly, I thank my mother, Maria Helena de Vasconcelos, who gave me so many of these stories and to whom this book belongs, and my father, Aurélio de Vasconcelos, whose love and kindness have made everything possible.

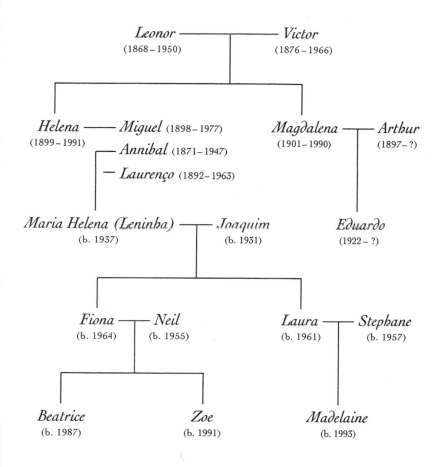

Prologue

I HAVE NOT COME TO
HEAR THEM SING

I am kneeling before my grandmother. Her thigh is as thick as my arm. She is sitting in her chair beside the bed, pulling on stockings. They are thick and woolly, like little girls' tights, and I must hold them up with an old elastic, a band she may have used before around some book, or a stack of letters. She is tiny, tiny. This is the chair she will die in, later, though we do not know it yet. About the chair, I mean. Death is expected. Wished for, almost. Yes. Wished for.

I have come here with my mother: an old villa in the town of Lousa. We are an hour's bus ride away from Lisbon, where the nursing homes are overcrowded, or too expensive. In the spring the yellow stucco must look beautiful, the town as quaint as any other Portuguese town, winding roads climbing out of valleys, houses stuck together as if there were a scarcity of space, though we are in the middle of the countryside. But it is winter now, grey and damp. The rooms are cold here, my feet are frozen.

I have come as support, to help my own mother watch her mother die, in this nursing home, at the age of ninety-three. My grandmother has only been here a few months, since my great-aunt died. Magdalena was her sister; the one who took care of her.

"And they all thought I would die first, you see, but I didn't!"

These are the first words my grandmother utters when told of Magdalena's death. She says it with anger, tearfully, like a child whose most valuable toy has been snatched away. My grandmother has spent her life being taken care of by servants, husbands, a sister. My mother, by virtue of geography, has been spared this task, until now. She has done the best she can under the circumstances. Given what was available. But my grandmother does not like it here. She is helpless, among strangers.

"I will die here, Leninha, I will die here if you do not take me out."

This seems strange, coming from a woman in her nineties, speaking of her own death as if it were still only a remote possibility.

"But Mother, there are so many nice ladies here!"

My mother looks about briskly, smiling, finding things to do. She is checking my grandmother's closet, editing. A stack of old cookie boxes emerges, uneaten. Clothes my grandmother has not worn.

"Mother, look at these beautiful gloves, they're brand new!"

"I don't use them."

"But they're so nice, Mother."

"Please, Leninha."

Two gloves at the bottom of a tin box. Notebooks, more elastics, an old watch. A lifetime of possessions condensed into this room. Reduced, that is. My grandmother looks into the box, half-curiously. She fingers a red pen and offers it to me. But as I stretch out my hand she says, "Oh, but you can't use it, you don't write Portuguese!"

These are the slips of her mind. I smile, and as I close the box she has a sudden memory: "Didn't one of them write, Leninha?"

"Of course, Mother. Fiona used to write. She wrote poems in school, remember?"

My grandmother begins to cry.

"Please, Leninha, don't move that table!"

She cannot bear change anymore. She cannot bear to be given a bath. My grandmother is tired of living. But she has no choice. We leave her for the day, sitting now in the main parlour, among the other ladies. She is holding with both hands the little black purse that she carries everywhere. In it is a notebook where she writes things to herself, in order to remember. That and a lipstick whose dark-pink colour matches exactly the tiny spot on the tip of my grandmother's nose.

The train stops in Sintra, an old, hilly town surrounded by forest. I am here on my mother's advice: "No sense in all three of us suffering," she says. "Go and enjoy yourself a little."

I have spent the ride from Lisbon thinking of Neil, feeling his face float above me as it did days ago, watching me pack as if he were daring me to. We have spent endless hours discussing this, my trip, its necessity, its inconvenience. I feel the required amount of guilt, leaving him alone in the middle of January; duty and pleasure matter equally, for the one that stays behind. Or perhaps it is not guilt, but fear.

"This is my last chance to see her alive," I tell him. "Besides, my mother needs me."

"What about your sister, can't she go?"

"Laura has that big exhibit coming up, you know that."

"Of course," he says. "You can do whatever you want, Fiona, I keep telling you, it's your life." Neil laughs quietly to himself, as if he were the only one astute enough to understand the joke: "Hey, you might even meet a handsome stranger."

"This is not about me, Neil."

"All right," he says. "Look, it'll probably do you good to get away."

Away from what is what I want to ask.

I follow the curving road that leads up to the castle at the top of the hill, a Moorish fantasy covered in thick tiles where the turrets and balconies jut out over Sintra's forests. They call it *O Castello da Pena*: the castle of sadness. It is raining and cold and almost deserted. The castle overlooks the palace, down below in the centre of town, with its twin chimneys and glorious rooms. Magdalena, my great-aunt, used to describe them often, retelling the story behind each room, her favourite a small bedroom at the top of a staircase where a deposed king spent the last nine years of his life, imprisoned by his own brother and wife. The room, as I remember it, contained nothing but a bed, a table and a window. But it was the stones of the floor, worn from nine years of pacing, which gave the story its poignancy. "Of course he went mad in the end," she would say. "Imagine, *querida*, nine years of betrayal and despair." Perhaps it was the palace that they should have called *Pena*.

I have brought my camera with me and I walk around taking pictures as if this were my sole purpose in visiting, acquiring a record that could justify my presence here with something more than the futile witnessing of my grandmother's death. Wet tiled terraces, moss-covered walls. A pigeon sitting on the edge of a pool. How beautiful it is, this place, this country. I had forgotten its smells, the sounds of its streets. Its age. As a child I had hated the grime, the dilapidation of its painted houses, so unlike the tidy, open country from which I came. Age is a kind of decadence; it never appeals to the very young, or the very old.

I climb up to the highest turret. On a clear day I could see the ocean from here, trace with my finger as on an ancient map the line that edges a continent, *where the earth ends and the sea begins*, as Camões wrote. But I am completely in mist. I take a picture of the whiteness.

My grandmother eats chocolates at night while saying her prayers. She has also never used deodorant on her armpits. Her secret is to scrub them with one of those wire kitchen sponges, the kind we use at home when burnt rice sticks to the bottom of the pan. I never try this method, thinking that it will not work for me. My grandmother's eccentricities are exclusive.

She has had three husbands: divorced one and outlived two. The first and last were the worst and best, I am told, but it is my grandmother's second marriage that interests me. I have a photograph of her husband, Annibal, in my album upstairs. I have never thought of him as my grandfather, because he dies when my mother is only ten. He is thirty years older than my grandmother, and wealthy. He does not start out as her husband, though. Out of wedlock, they call it, and very daring in the 1930s. They only marry after my mother is born. On the day of his death my mother looks at herself in the mirror and smiles.

"He never said a kind word to me in my life," she says.

"Annibal was a very stern man," my grandmother says, "but at seventy-six he could satisfy any woman."

I don't know if this means quantity or quality. Still, the woman's need is acknowledged, which is in itself surprising.

I know full well that my grandmother never loved Annibal. She speaks of him as though she were describing a moment in history, like some war with its attendant sacrifices. A moment that was endured, necessary, inevitable; not that bad, in the end. My grandmother has no regrets. The real love of her life is a man whom she never marries, who has a family of his own. A descendant of princes, I am told, though we only find this out much later. By a series of special circumstances my mother discovers, at age forty, who her real father is. A great secret has been kept by my grandmother all these years. A secret unveiled. We are somewhat proud of this story in my family. It adds colour.

"Every woman has a moment of passion in her life," my grandmother says.

Passion. The glamour of it obscures everything. Particularly pain.

We sit at the Lião d'Ouro, my mother and I, laughing and eating. We have spent the day shopping, spoiling ourselves with new shoes and jewellery. Earrings, covered in marcasites.

Back home people will ask us, "Are they antique?" and sometimes we will lie and say yes, yes they are. It is dinner time now, and we are very giggly. I have spilt a glass of red wine all over the table, annoying the waiters and the couple beside us. Someone laughs: a grey-bearded man sitting by himself at a corner table. He raises his glass towards us and smiles.

My mother raises her eyebrows. "You know what they say, Fiona, change is as good as rest."

"Don't be silly, Mom."

"There aren't many virtuous women in your ancestry, darling; you might not want to break with tradition."

"Will you stop it?"

We laugh. A respite, this, especially for my mother. She has gone to visit my grandmother every day, listened to her whimpers and complaints, tried to make it bearable. It is unbearable, for both of them. My mother takes her out to the local café, one day, as a special treat.

"But I thought you were taking me to Lisbon," my grandmother cries, "my dear, dear Lisbon——"

"She'll do just fine," my mother says suddenly. "She's in a good place. Que remedio?"

In the curve of my mother's shoulders is the outline of my grandmother's back.

"She's lived her life, Mom, she made her own choices."

"One day you'll understand this, Fiona, because we'll be in this same place again; you'll be in *my* place. I never thought I could be so hard, so cruel, but she did it to me, you know, she brought me up hard. You only see the frail little old lady. You remember her from those beautiful photographs, from all those stories. Her marriages. Her men. She's always had that ability, to make herself helpless. They all found it so alluring. I used to come to her, when I was little, with some question or other, anything to get her attention, and she would tell me to go and see if she was in the other room. As if I was stupid, can you imagine? And then she shipped me off to the convent school right after Annibal's death, and left me there for six years. It wouldn't have mattered whether I was happy in that place or not. It was simply luck that I was."

"Didn't you miss her?"

"I remember lying in the dormitory at night, listening to the other girls crying, and I felt jealous of them. I wanted to have someone to cry for. One day she came to see me act in a play. I played a duck. You'll never be an actress, she said. *Pow*. Just like that."

"Did you love her?"

"I told her once, when I was at the convent and only twelve, that I wished she could enter my body, like Christ in communion. What nonsense, she said."

Obidos, in full sun. Another outing for me, this medieval town surrounded by thick stone walls. In sunlight they are the colour of honey, and within them the tiny whitewashed houses have their shutters and windowsills painted blue. To ward off the evil spirits, they say. I have been walking all morning along the top of the wall and through the streets. I have been walking with the deliberate pace of someone who knows that she is being followed.

We have played this game for a while now, he and I.

It is dangerous, but also exciting. From the start I have recognized him, the grey-haired man from the restaurant, who laughed at my spilt wine. He wears yellow pants and a turquoise sweater. But it's tiring, this game of peek-a-boo. It opens up the appetite.

I stop at a restaurant, a small room, really, with a few tables and a doorway leading to the kitchen at the back. The air smells of bread and olive oil, and the woman who brings me my food is also the one who has prepared it. Before long he is sitting across from me, pouring the wine and offering me tastes from his plate. We talk in sign language, improvising, because he speaks only Italian.

"Bella, bella," he keeps repeating.

"Thank you," I say.

He has one eye blue and one eye green.

The room is nearly empty by the time we have finished.

"I must go," I tell him.

"Go," he says. "Bene."

I try to show him my watch, explaining about buses and schedules, but he takes my hand and begins pulling me along the streets, towards the edge of the town, towards the wall. Do I risk this? Do I give in? I try to think of Neil, of his smile, of his eyes on that first day, when he told me that I was beautiful. I feel the rough stones of the wall, warm from the sun, pressing against my back.

I run away from him, from Obidos, stopping only to wash my face at a water fountain, wishing I could wash away the dampness from in between my legs. It was not the taste of his mouth that scared me, but the unabashed helplessness with which his whole body said *I beg you.*

My grandmother is dead. Her death comes not as a shock; only the timing has surprised us. We had not expected to find ourselves here, at the cemetery. Not this time. Not yet. But we stand here, along with a few others who knew my grandmother, watching as two men dig a hole in the ground, a hole big enough to contain her body and her coffin. As they toss the earth to one side a bone flies through the air, landing with a white thump beside the open grave. My mother does not flinch, seeing this. But later, when she thinks of my grandmother, it is not the arrogant, beautiful woman she remembers, nor the silent mother who tiptoed into her room one night and placed three tiny kisses on her upturned wrist, thinking she was asleep, nor the bent old lady who sat quietly in her chair as my mother turned down the bed, in a room which was never my grandmother's room, and said only, "I think I am wet."

What she remembers is the bone.

April. My mother and I have been back in Montreal for three months now, each to our own home and husband. I have been making beds, cooking dinner. Neil has taken to telling me that he loves me, lately. He does this with great seriousness and some humility, as if he were presenting an offering to some long dead saint. I have no reason to doubt the sincerity of these three words, *I love you,* though I am beginning to glimpse life without Neil as a possibility.

My mother has given me a basket with some of my grandmother's things. ("Too much for me to keep," she says.) In it are a pair of earrings, her glasses, her watch and the little notebook that she carried around in her purse. The last written page has only three lines: my mother's name, the phone number of our hotel in Lisbon and, further down below, in careful, crooked letters, the word *confusa*.

I am confused.

My mother has also given me another gift, another relic from these two deaths: Magdalena's memoirs, blue ink on loose-leaf, gathered in a plastic binder. I have placed them on the top shelf of my closet under a stack of sweaters. They wait to be read. But I have kept my grandmother's notebook in my purse, in the silk-lined pocket that closes with a zipper like the secret compartments I used to love as a little girl. I carry it with me now as I enter the church on Notre Dame square. It is windy outside. I have been long and hard at finding a parking spot. I hadn't expected the church to be crowded. I haven't come for prayer. The front of the church is filled with girls in pleated skirts, a uniform from some private school, like I wore too, once. A nun jerks and twitches before them.

"Sing, girls, sing!"

I have not come to hear them sing. I haven't come to tell Him that I am no longer innocent. That I might have fucked a stranger and liked it, with the sun shining on the cobblestones as we did it.

I haven't come to tell Him that I believe.

I find a seat beside an old woman with oily hair and dusty nails, who farts twice out loud. She tapes the singing voices and I like her.

I have not come to hear them sing. I have not come to cry beside a putrid-smelling woman.

I walk outside the church and watch the pigeons sit on

Champlain's shoulders. They are oblivious, these birds, oblivious as the old man who makes this square his home, year after year, carrying a huge vinyl bag and wearing an old silk cap on his head. He smiles at me with total ease, as if we both inhabit the same universe. I think of my grandmother with her chocolates and prayers. It occurs to me that despite all she went through, she had always remained healthy. At ninety-two her only ailment was an eye that had too many tears. They would pop up at the oddest moments. She always had a handkerchief to wipe them away.

I

BALZAC'S HEAD

This is a house of many rooms. Magdalena's house. She has lived in it for eighty-seven years. She calls it a house but it is really a flat, like all houses in Lisbon, with a dozen or so rooms strung along a corridor, forming a horseshoe. She occupies the third story of an old building where the floors are wooden and dull from wear; they creak loudly, as loudly as the stairs which wind up the centre of the building, announcing any visitors well before they have time to reach her door. This is just as well; Magdalena's keyhole is as large as an olive.

Many rooms stand empty now because an old lady can occupy only so much space. Many things have been sold off over the years, given away, forgotten. Magdalena has been shedding her possessions, growing lighter with the passing of time. But she prides herself on the uses to which she has put some rooms: the laundry room with its ironing-board and folding table always set up, extremely practical, she admits; the luggage room where she keeps all her suitcases; even a telephone room, a resurrection from her youth when the invention was still so new it stood cloistered in its own special place, still unassimilated into the realm of commonplace objects.

Then of course there are the usual rooms, an antiquated kitchen and a dining-room, a parlour filled with books and worn-out upholstery, old photographs in silver frames and coloured postcards from the 1950s stuck to the wall. Magdalena's taste runs from the tacky to the sublime. One bedroom now belongs to Magdalena's sister, Helena, who comes to stay reluctantly, whenever she is ill. And on the happiest and rarest occasions, such as today, the other rooms are occupied by Leninha and her two daughters, Laura and Fiona. They have come to spend part of their holiday in Lisbon, where they will shop and take in a few sights.

"You may find the beds a little lumpy, I'm afraid," Magdalena says. "This is like coming from Paradise to purgatory!"

Laura and Fiona will politely deny Magdalena's claim, because they are old enough to appreciate the quaintness of age.

"What a great place," they will say.

Embracing their slim, brown bodies, she takes them into her house, filling it and herself with laughter, conversation, confusion. She knows they will not stay long, returning as they should to the hotels of Cascais and Estoril where she will be invited to spend afternoons, sipping water and tea on the *Esplanada* by the beach. But in her own house she tells them stories. They listen to her with the curiosity of the young.

When they leave, Magdalena is less merry, but not sentimental. She stands on the stone threshold of her building, by the bottom of the stairs, keeping open with her shoulder the old front door, which is black and has a tendency to slam shut, as in the closing of a vault. The building had a porter many years ago, who would open the door from inside at any time of the day or night. Magdalena's mother used to summon him by clapping her hands in the darkened street whenever she returned from the theatre, or the opera. None of the other residents have been here long enough to remember him.

Magdalena holds up her palm, waving it like a salute. She is crying, but has a smile on her face.

"This passes," she says. "This passes."

"I have written down everything," she says, "so that you know. It's all here. In my memoirs."

Magdalena rests her hand on a binder thick with papers. She is showing them her desk, a seventeenth-century antique where she keeps all the records of her life. Inside one of the drawers is a little note pasted with tape, yellowed now to a deep, brittle orange.

This desk was given to me by my father-in-law, Antonio Lopes Ferreira, in the year of my wedding. It was very old, even then, and thought to have come from India.

In this way Magdalena has catalogued all her possessions. One has to know the history of things, she says, otherwise they have no meaning. She passes this down to them, this love of objects, handing out gifts at each of their visits. A painted teacup, a brooch encrusted with diamonds, a tiny book bound in silk still bearing the names of young men waiting for a dance at the next ball. Bits of *her* history. Laura and Fiona will carry them back to their young country with pride, with reverence almost, knowing how important they are. Because they have lasted this long. Because like the walls of her house, they may carry some of Magdalena's spirit. Because possibly — or so they hope — some of it might rub off.

The most important room in Magdalena's house, her bedroom, fills one tip of the horseshoe. Like the parlour at the opposite end it has intricate ceilings and rounded corners, and windows on two sides. She has painted the walls a mustard colour, climbing on stepladders. The colour reminds her of Rome, she says, her favourite city. Only Magdalena remembers what the room may have looked like, long ago, when it was still her mother's. She can recall precisely the sound of her father's footsteps walking towards the door every second night, like clockwork, at the same hour, and smiles thinking back to other nights, when the pattern of his footsteps ended at another door down the hall, near the kitchen. Magdalena has always been a light sleeper. She often spends hours sitting bolt upright on her bed, looking at the night table where Leonor, her mother, would sometimes find love letters. Magdalena has recounted the anecdote often:

"Poor Daddy. He had written to some other lady, but sent the letters to his own address! Mother simply placed them on his desk without uttering a single word." Magdalena laughs. Laura and Fiona are meant to understand by this that they come from a long line of strong women.

The room became hers in 1922. She would occupy it with Arthur, a man of twenty-five from a good family who had courted her with roses and boxed chocolates. After the wedding her parents had moved to a smaller flat, leaving Magdalena to her first night with a stranger. Who could have known that Arthur's greatest quality would turn out to be a love of card games and fine silk scarves? Like that of many others, his presence in the house would only be temporary. But long enough to cause real damage.

"Nothing is worse than a ruined marriage," Magdalena says. "I entered that church wearing a veil that was as white as my illusions. I think that was the only day in my life when I looked truly beautiful, climbing up the wide front steps with the sun shining on my veil. How blind I was, like all the girls of my time. It was a game of chance, really, you won or you lost."

Magdalena will not dwell on this, the strange force that compels two people to join each other in order to suffer. She will not dwell on past pain, nor mourn the loss of a girl who walked towards the church door, in the bright sunlight of an August morning, as another bride, just married, stepped out. But she may recall, with a clarity that still stings, the words of the woman in the guest party who'd said, watching the two brides cross each other, "One of them will be unhappy."

Magdalena tells a story.

"He was without question the greatest leader of the nineteenth century. A brilliant man. You know, *querida*, I always say the world needs a good dictator now and then, not like those spineless idiots we have nowadays. Salazar was no angel, but in some ways we were better off back then. Today we have the blind leading the blind. But Napoleon. To have come from nothing—— Did you know that he crowned himself emperor? Yes, yes, I'm very fond of Napoleon——"

She is talking history again. Her passion, she says, along with travelling. She has spent a large part of her life walking throughout Europe, soaking up the stories of each country, down to the last king who fought the last battle, or stood behind the castle walls, waiting. Hers is the history of anecdote, though she stands proudly behind her knowledge of facts. She can recall names and dates with the precision of an encyclopaedia, and rattles them off laughing, pleased with herself. She has travelled the cities and found herself among groups of people following tour guides with the matchless attention of those who know nothing, and will soon forget what they have heard. She has often, in fact, usurped the poor cicerones whose unfortunate mistake it was to merely approximate a date, or designate a painted lady as "unknown."

"Let me tell you something, young man. There are no unknowns. Unknowns only exist for those of us who are too lazy or too ignorant to care. Did you know that Napoleon had a sister? This is her portrait."

No doubt she charmed them all, as she charms them now, an old lady of eighty-seven years, who memorizes the social security number of all her friends, just for the fun of it. Who paints her bedroom walls mustard, climbing on stepladders. Who loves Napoleon for the sheer strength of his will, for his arrogance. Never mind that he killed hundreds of thousands. Like Magdalena, he was very short, but never had any complaints on that account.

Magdalena is lying on her bed wearing a black-lace bra and stockings, pulling on something at her navel. She hears her grandniece Fiona walking along the corridor, looking for her shoes. Magdalena doesn't have them, but calls out just the same. Fiona opens the door without knocking and stands speechless for a moment, shocked as if she had intruded on some unspeakable act.

"I'm sorry, Auntie, I was looking for my shoes ——"

"For heaven's sake, *querida*, come and help me with this girdle," Magdalena says.

The last time Magdalena sees her lover, Alberto, he is already very ill. The large tumour that has grown on the side of his face since she has known him has finally spread, eating away at other things. He has become thin, a shadow of himself; he can barely make the stairs. He has come to say goodbye, to spend a few last hours before going home. He will not come again, and they both know it. And she will not go and visit him. His death belongs to his family, of which she is not a part. They have been lovers for twenty-five years.

Alberto is married, of course; he is a man of means. A Supreme Court judge. Magdalena is the love of his life and he has kept her at his side, all these years, taken her everywhere. Her house has been his at all times of the day or night. But a man in his position cannot relinquish everything, and he has kept up appearances, for his own sake and that of his wife. She has accommodated, held onto his name and his children, wrapping them around herself like furs, like the fur-collared coats that he brings her from his travels, cities he has walked with Magdalena on his arm. She has understood, accepted. Set herself in that place he has allowed for, that little place. Perhaps she loves him still, or has a lover of her own. Hers is another story.

Magdalena does not ask Alberto about his wife, his children, the other half of his life. She feels no jealousy, and very little guilt. She has made sacrifices of her own, wondering at times how she will get through the last hours of the day without him. She has even aborted his children, on more than one occasion, knowing how much an illegitimate child would cost him. (One can only push the boundaries of scandal so far.) But she has also sat in his courtroom, through all the celebrated murder cases at which he presides, and watched him order a little universe like a god. She knows who he is, the imposing man at the front. She knows his temper, his fits of jealousy. She has held him in her arms when he was afraid, moments when he has begged her not to leave him. And it is enough.

Maria da Graça has lived in Magdalena's house for thirty years. She has been a maid since she was fifteen, worked for Magdalena's parents and then their daughter, from sunrise until ten, with every other Sunday off. She knows this house like her own body, has been witness to all the great events that have taken place in these rooms: the births, deaths, marriages, the passions and rages. And largely the mundane: the cooking, the scrubbing, the opening and closing of windows. The pieces that have made up Magdalena's life. Not Maria da Graça's life, but somehow hers, for she has had no other. One day she will tell Magdalena how she feels, how she has resented her, a woman who has had husband, lover and child, while *she* has had nothing. Magdalena will be astonished.

"I never knew Maria da Graça had such a mean streak in her," she will say. "Imagine being jealous of me all those years!"

But this moment is a long way off, and today they are just as they have always been, happy partners, not quite sisters, not quite friends. They are cleaning out the dining-room, sorting out the chipped china, the tablecloths that need mending. Collecting a pile for the garbage. Leninha and the girls have gone, and Magdalena must keep busy. On top of the buffet sits a large bust of Balzac, marble, with bulging eyes and chiselled brows.

"I've never liked his face," says my great-aunt. "Let's get rid of him."

"Are you sure, *menina*, he's not even chipped."

"He's too ugly, really. Such a huge head. But we won't throw poor Balzac away. Let's see who picks him up."

This is an old game of theirs, setting some object out on the street, watching from the window. They carry poor Balzac down the stairs, the two of them, because he is not only ugly but heavy. And then Maria da Graça lugs him to the corner, sits him carefully on the edge of the sidewalk and hurries back to the house. They wait. Soon enough Senhor Umberto appears. Magdalena knows him like all her other neighbours, his name and face, the essential details of his life. He is out walking this morning, as he does every Thursday, because Fernanda has come to clean the flat. His wife will not have him home on such days, watching Fernanda on her hands and knees. And he complies, as he does in all things. He has long since given up fighting her.

But few people would guess this, watching him walk

down the street, a large, portly, well-dressed man. He spots the bust from a few feet away, around the corner; he has already passed it when the thought occurs to him. He is puzzled. He goes on walking for a few metres, checks his watch, turns around.

"Look, it's Senhor Umberto!" whispers Maria da Graça.

He does this a few times, walking up and down the street, pausing at the grocer's, gazing up at windows. Finally, passing Balzac's head, heaves him up under one arm, hurrying home. His heart is beating. Who knows what his wife might say.

Upstairs, behind the curtain, Magdalena sits with her maid and laughs and laughs.

In this house of many rooms, the lights are usually on. Magdalena doesn't care for dark spaces, knowing she will have enough darkness in the coffin, when she gets there. She keeps the tall shutters open, letting in light and noise, the rumble of tires on cobblestones and the cranking of the garbage truck which passes twice weekly in the early hours of the morning. Magdalena always sets hers out the night before, expecting that it will have been picked through before dawn, for nothing is ever truly abandoned in these old countries.

In her old desk by the door are the sheets of paper she has been writing for years, now, her memoirs. She will keep these until the end, along with her two most sacred objects: Alberto's gold pocket watch, and the small bust of Napoleon that he kept on his desk. Alberto's son had brought them to her in the week following his father's death, along with a bank-account number ensuring that she would live comfortably until her death.

"We felt you should have them," the young man had said, "after all."

"Yes, my darling," she says.

Magdalena's voice echoes through the tall ceilings, a trail of conversations behind her head. She is not done yet.

II

SISTERS I (MONSTER FACE)

Montreal, Canada, 1988.

Fiona's legs are in stirrups. The nurse standing beside her is named Roz. Roz wears a plastic cap on her head similar to the ones Fiona used to see hanging in her mother's shower, when she was a girl. The room is covered in green tiles and the air is very cold, even the light from the disc-shaped fixture above the bed seems glacial. Fiona has read somewhere that the colour green rests surgeons' eyes.

Around the room are two or three other nurses, puttering cheerfully. The doctor greets them collectively when he enters: "Good morning, girls."

Roz takes hold of Fiona's hand and says, "Look into my eyes, dear. Let's go somewhere together, shall we?"

"This will only take a few minutes," the doctor says.

"Where should we go?" Roz asks.

"I don't know."

"All right, I'll choose. Let's go to Bali. We are walking on a beautiful beach——"

But there is a sudden sharp pain and she cannot listen anymore.

"Look into my eyes, Fiona. It will be over very soon. I'm going to give you something very soon. It's almost over."

She cannot open her eyes.

"No, not yet," says the doctor. "I'm sorry, not yet."

Finally, when the tearing has stopped, he holds a little cup filled with blood, holds it up between her legs, under the light, and examines it carefully.

"Would you like some orange juice, dear?"

Fiona stares at the green walls. Her teeth are clenched. She remembers now, green is the complementary of red.

When she sees them for the first time it is as if someone has punched her in the stomach. The dolls are hung on the wall from hooks, each one spaced exactly four feet apart, three on each wall. The legs and arms are limp. The heads droop slightly, left or right. They are hung at eye level, so that you see them straight on. Flesh-coloured dolls, embroidered faces, some of them have an eye or half a mouth missing. The bellies are rounded, like babies' bellies. They are meant to be babies, she guesses. Around the necks, shoulders and groins the seams are very visible, stitched in dark, glossy thread, some of them baseball-stitched. Like wounds that have been sewn closed.

The room is aglow with praise. Fiona sees Laura in the corner, the centre in a circle of people. For as long as she can remember she has seen her sister like this, surrounded. Laura is smiling, poised as always, elegant, even. She has spent months on these dolls, stuffing and stitching them. They are as detailed as any of those old tablecloths she has inherited. Must be something in the genes, this flair for embroidery.

Murmurs of praise flutter throughout the air and Fiona takes a deep breath. She feels the veins in her neck pulsing, the beginnings of a tight fist at the base of her skull. She makes her way through the crowded room, pauses now and then and tries to look at the dolls, can't help but avert her eyes. She kisses Laura on both cheeks.

"It's quite a turnout," she says.

"Yes," says Laura. "Where's Neil?"

"We couldn't get a sitter," Fiona says. "He stayed home with Bea."

"Would you like something to drink?"

"No, sorry. I can't stay long. I promised I'd put Bea to bed."

"I thought Neil was with her."

"Well, yes, but I promised I'd be back in time."

Laura attempts a smile. "So, what do you think?"

"I don't know what to think, Laura. When you said dolls...I didn't expect this."

"It wouldn't be art if it was predictable, Fiona."

"That's not what I meant."

"No, I guess it wasn't."

"I'm sure you'll do very well with the show," Fiona says. "I have to go."

A kiss on both cheeks again and Fiona walks out of the gallery. She is wearing a red coat and clutching a furry scarf at her neck. Fiona is perennially cold. Outside the air is heavy with dampness, the streets are black and wet. Fiona drives south along St-Denis street, passing the old building that housed Laura's first apartment. Right in the middle of where everything is at, Laura had said, describing it. Fiona

remembers visiting with her parents that first time, feign-
ing delight at the tall, cracked walls, the high windows, the
claw-footed tub.

"Isn't it great, Daddy, isn't it amazing?"

Resigned chuckles all around. ("Que mess, que mess,"
her mother had whispered.)

Fiona had walked through the rooms and looked out
of the windows. She would have this too, she thought, she
would do better than this, when the time came. She would
have plants on the windowsills and sunlight pouring through
lace. Laura and Stephane had placed two candles on a bedside table, and the sight of these hurt her most of all. Looking at the blackened wicks and pools of beaded wax Fiona
knew that her sister was happy.

It had been worth it, then, for Laura, the great struggle to leave home, the disappointment it had caused everyone. The first daughter leaving the nest, an event her parents
had looked forward to as something grand, a little bit
solemn, with every box deliberately and slowly packed,
with her room changed and even empty — they would have
expected that — with a suitcase coming down the stairs last
of all. Their father, Joaquim, had stood by the front door,
watching Laura and Stephane stuff the car, bags and crum-
pled boxes piled high.

"Playing house, that's what this is," he'd said. "Just playing house."

He would have liked the suitcase on the stair, the sound
of church bells. Not this lifeless leaving, the absence of for-
mal goodbyes. She would not give him that, but he would
forgive her. Joaquim would forgive his daughters anything.

Fiona had stayed home, relieved. Harmony had descended on the house again, and she had waited her turn, done things the expected way. A white wedding, a choir of singing children. An Ave Maria no one could forget. She has lit some candles of her own, since then, with Neil. She keeps a pair by the sunken tub at home, in crystal candle holders. Quite exquisite, but dripless. She has used them, once or twice.

"I am Igor, your faithful servant," says Fiona, her head trapped tightly in the crook of Laura's arm, down by her waist. They often walk around like this, the two of them, with Laura dragging Fiona every which way, turning sharply, laughing as her bent sister struggles to catch up, following the trail of her own head like a dog on a leash. The game is much tougher on sand, and Fiona stumbles. She is laughing and screaming at the same time.

"You're hurting me!"

"Shut up, Igor, or I'll throw you in the dungeon, where all the bugs are!"

"Stop it!"

"Stop it! Stop it! Cry baby!"

Fiona can't help but laugh, her sister is so funny. Laura's face is elastic, she turns it into the greatest monsters, at the worst moments. It is maddening, this inability to stay angry. It enrages her every time. She clutches at some sand now and throws it in Laura's direction.

"I'm telling!" Laura says.

Leninha and Joaquim are sitting beside one of the many striped tents that line the beach. They are sipping wine and

laughing with a group of people, Joaquim's brothers and
their spouses, a nephew, Carlos, and his wife, Celeste, who
are contemplating a move to Canada.

"It's a completely different life," Leninha is explaining.
"Things are so much easier in North America."

"Mommy, Fiona threw sand in my face."

"I did not!"

"But you still come back for this," says Amândio, gesturing towards the sea. Amândio is Joaquim's youngest brother,
and the favourite uncle in the family. He is very good at
practical jokes and usually spends his holiday with Joaquim
and Leninha when they visit Portugal. Fiona and Laura have
often heard Leninha say that if she hadn't married their
father, she would have married Amândio.

"She did too!"

The two little girls stand side by side, facing their
mother. Laura is ten years old, three years older than Fiona,
and already has breasts. A lovely little waist, hips that will
stay with her, unchanged, for the next forty years, through
men and children even. Fiona's breasts are called two raisins
on a bread box, a phrase that follows wherever she goes.

"Come on, girls," Leninha says.

Amândio reaches out for Fiona suddenly, and starts
tickling her. "What are you complaining about, kid, look at
you, wearing this bikini. You don't need a bikini, you're just
a baby! Don't you know that babies go naked on the beach
in Portugal?"

He pulls at her bikini top and unhooks the straps, starts
running with it dangling from his hand.

"Two raisins on a bread box!" Laura says.

Fiona chases after him, crying and laughing again, a flat-chested kid trying to be womanly.

"Give it back!"

"All right, all right!"

Amândio falls to the ground as if he were sorely defeated. By the tent, Fiona's parents are laughing gaily. She stares at them with burning eyes and stomps off.

The beach is fairly crowded, and Fiona meanders around several families before reaching the water. Around her are all the beach sounds, mothers chasing their children with offerings of food, the squeals of warm bodies immersing in cold water, the calling out of vendors selling sweets and ice-cream, their voices trailing up and down the beach in a rhythmic chant. These vendors are one of the few things Fiona truly likes about Portugal. They carry with them the warm pastries that her mother buys each morning, soft, giant balls of dough covered in white sugar in which Fiona sinks her teeth: the taste of happiness.

The sea is rough today and so has given up more of its treasures than usual. Fiona squats and begins to gather rocks and bits of glass, each piece worn smooth and round. A few bits of clay are covered in tiny holes, marinelike, ancient. Fiona licks the salt off some of them.

It feels as if she has been working for hours when Amândio finds her. She has gathered more than she could carry in two hands.

"How's it going, beauty?" he says.

Fiona doesn't answer. Amândio has a bucket in his hand.

"You know, if you put those stones in the oven over-night, they will turn to gold."

Fiona lifts up her eyes. "They will not," she says.

"I'm serious. Don't you believe me?"

"How do you know?" she asks.

Amândio holds out the bucket. "Because I know things that no one else knows," he says, smiling.

Sunday dinner. Everyone standing around the kitchen, the food is almost ready. Fiona's daughter Beatrice is dancing on the floor, with "Itsy Bitsy Spider" playing on the tape recorder.

"I'm so sick of that song!" says Leninha, teasing.

Neil is flipping through a week-old *Time* magazine. Fiona dances with her daughter, Leninha cooks. Laura and Stephane are opening up a can of oysters.

"I just don't know if I want to sell the entire collection," Laura says. "I'm not sure if I want them on permanent display like that."

"Where would they put them?" Leninha asks.

"In a conference room."

"In a way it's more powerful that way, don't you think, Laura?"

"I'm not sure."

"A conference room?" asks Fiona.

"It would mean a lot of money, anyway. It's unlikely that I would sell them all individually."

"That's not a minor consideration," offers Joaquim.

"Why would anyone want to work in a room surrounded by dead, naked babies?"

"Some people like to be surrounded by art, Fiona."

"Yes, of course," Fiona says. "I completely forgot about art!"

"What's that supposed to mean?"

"Nothing, Laura. Not a damn thing."

"Can we have a civil conversation around this dinner table, for once?" asks Joaquim.

"They're just having a discussion, honey, let them talk, for heaven's sake!"

"Here we go again," Neil mutters.

Beatrice sits on her grandfather's lap, watching him peel an orange.

"Find me a baby one, Grandpa," she says.

"I used to do that, remember? I would eat an orange and Mom would find the little piece, tucked in next to the big one, and say it was the baby. I always saved them on the edge of my plate, as if they were too good to eat, remember?"

"You always ate them in the end," Laura says.

"Thanks, Laura. Would you like to turn that into a piece of great art as well? You could stick little pieces of orange onto pins and hang them around a room and it would be very profound, don't you think? Is there anything else of mine that you'd like to appropriate?"

Laura stares at her sister. "One day, Fiona, one day you're going to wake up. And when you do you'll ask yourself where you've been all these years."

"You don't know a single thing about me," Fiona says. "Find your own bloody tragedies to work on."

"That's right. Some of us *work*, Fiona."

"Where's Mommy going?" asks Beatrice.

"We could have had such a nice dinner," says Leninha.

Fiona's father kisses little Bea on the temple and passes her to Neil. He walks to the front of the house, stands behind the living-room window in time to watch Fiona rush down the stairs, struggling with her coat. He has witnessed so many of these, the fights between his two daughters. He has stood at their adolescent bedsides, holding hands and patting heads, waiting for the rages to subside. He is helpless now, as then. He cannot understand them. But he watches as his daughter turns the corner. The roads are icy. He hopes she gets home safe.

Fiona opens her eyes. A band of yellow light dances at the base of the curtain so it must be morning. The house is very still and Fiona steps quietly, bare feet on the cool, stone floor. She walks into the kitchen, a little girl in a white nightgown, her body still warm from sleep. Her uncle is sitting at the table, a cup between his hands.

"Is it morning?" he says.

"I think so."

"You'd better check, then."

Fiona pulls gingerly on the oven door. There, floating in the centre of a deep black box, are two dozen pieces of gold.

"Mommy! Mommy!" Fiona squeals. "Mommy come and see!"

The rest of the house wakes.

Fiona runs the bath, the long oval tub that she keeps scrupulously clean, filling it almost halfway before she even gets in. A luxury for her, this, she so seldom gets to lie here alone, without Bea. But she has some time now, before they get back. She can let the needles in her feet turn to warmth.

She will soak here and try to think of nothing, let her

mind drift. Her skin is red, the water is so hot. She looks down at her stomach, places her hands on the loosened skin. Her body is empty, empty. She closes her eyes.

Suddenly she is standing on the toilet seat, her body wet, gasping for air. She is trying to scream, but no sound comes out, no air goes in. Her mother is there, in front of her, pounding her back. She, too, is scared, but her face is obscured, blurred by Fiona's own terror. Laura sits in the bathtub, watching. They have played this game so often, nothing has ever happened before.

And then it is over, a door opens, the air comes through. Fiona is crying now, deep sobs, catching up on all the breathing she has missed.

"All right," says her mother, "you didn't drown. You just swallowed a bit of water."

In the tub, Laura is rinsing her long hair.

"You didn't die," she says. "Stop acting like a baby."

But she has died. The possibility of death has become real to her. She will even pretend to die, a few days later, to see how it feels again. She lies under the water in the bathtub, hands and head floating limp, waiting for her sister's hand on the doorknob, for the voice that says, "Push over, I want to get in." She has no idea how cruel she is being. Death seems a little funny, somehow. Until she hears Laura's voice calling her, Fiona, Fiona, calling her back from the dead. This is a different kind of terror.

Laura and Stephane sit in the old Volvo they have recently bought. It is below freezing, and they have had to jump start it again. The car jerks forward, accelerates, stops again.

"You're going to ruin the gears, Laura."

"I hate this car. I've hated it from the very beginning. I don't know why we bought it."

"Would you prefer a Ford Taurus, dear?"

"Very funny," she says.

"T."

"Ford Taurus."

"What starts with O?"

"Oldsmobile."

"Think of a car that starts with the letter C."

"C? C . . . Chevy."

"H."

"Honda."

"With a P."

"Porsche."

"Great, Laura. You're doing great."

Fiona is lying on the bed with her sister, it is close to dinner time. They have been playing a word game. Soon their mother will walk into the room, tray in hand, and the pleading will begin, the begging for Laura to eat. Laura has been in this bed for three weeks now, practically unable to move. She says she has a pain in her head, a horrible pain. Meal times are the worst, when Fiona watches her try to swallow, Laura's hand clutching her own neck as if it were about to snap in two. She has lost fifteen pounds.

None of the doctors seem to know what is wrong, despite the battery of tests. Laura insists: somewhere in the recesses of her brain there is a tumour. The doctors can't find it. They have told her to go home.

"We'll find another doctor, dear," her parents say. "Sometimes you just have to shop around."

But Fiona knows. She knows that there is no tumour, no physical illness. Only a gigantic fear which is tearing her sister open, taking bits of her away, leaving her small and thin. And so Fiona plays the letter game with Laura, over and over, watching her sister's body closely, waiting for the trembling to stop. Eventually, it does stop.

"You shouldn't let her get to you," Neil says, finding his wife in the bathroom, sitting in a tub of cold water.

"You shouldn't let her get to you," says Stephane, watching his wife fight the steering wheel, a lip between her teeth.

Fiona returns to the gallery. There is no one in the room, at first. The dolls look different in daylight, deflated, somehow, more fragile. They remind her of an old Raggedy Ann she once had, a doll that had survived pen marks and scissors and innumerable Band-Aids. Fiona reaches out and touches one of them, joining the tip of her finger to a nose, an eye, a mouth.

"Oh. It's you," Laura says. "I was downstairs."

"Sorry. I should have knocked, or something."

"It's OK."

"I thought I'd see them once again, before you dismantle the show."

"That's nice."

"So, what did you decide, finally?"

"I don't know if I'll sell any of them," Laura says. "I think I might just hang onto them for a while."

"Oh. I'm sorry, Laura."

Laura's eyes are dark.

"Bea looked really adorable, the other night," she says. "You're an amazing mother, Fiona."

Fiona looks away. "We're so different," she says.

"It's OK," Laura says. "It's OK that we are different."

Fiona looks at the dolls. "Can I have one?" she says suddenly. "To keep, I mean?"

Laura smiles. "Yeah. Just don't hang it in the living-room, all right?"

Fiona steps towards the wall and lifts one of the dolls from its hook, easy. Outside, she tucks the doll under her coat. It is light as a feather, she can barely feel it against her body, light as a bean floating in water. That baby would have taken up too much space. There was so little left of her already, after Neil and Bea. She hadn't expected it to be so all-consuming... A baby that she had decided, *she* had decided to abort. The one she wasn't ready for. *A bean*, that's what the technician had called it, pointing to the ultrasound. A bean missing in a little red cup, in a green room with cheerful nurses and a doctor saying *we're gonna have to do another one*. Twice she had killed it, that baby. The thing just didn't want to die. She had lain in the hospital bed in recovery, after the second time, next to a boy who had had surgery of some kind.

"You must lie down," the nurses kept telling him.

The boy had slanted eyes and thick features and he would not lie down. Fiona wondered if he could feel anything.

Neil had driven her home, later, and made her some toast.

"Where's Bea?" she had asked.

"I took her to your mom's; she'll be back later."

She had lain frozen in their bed clutching a hot-water bottle, remembering the slew of gloved hands that had entered her.

"Please don't turn the heating off," she'd said.

"I won't, darling, I promise."

Do you mind if I take a look? The sac is intact. Take a deep breath now. I'm afraid it didn't work, the abortion didn't work. I love you. How are you, Fiona? I'm going to give you something very soon, dear. What do you mean, it didn't work? It's your decision, darling, I'm not inside your body. Do you mind if I take a look? Would you like some orange juice, dear? I love you. Yes. Can you stand up by yourself, or shall I stay? I have to go to the bathroom. I'll be here, just press the button if you need me. Good luck. Thank you.

The following morning she had walked into the bathroom on shaky legs and watched the drops of blood hit the tiled floor, and she had thought, *that blood is too red.* But she had recovered and gone Christmas shopping, taken her daughter to visit Santa Claus, forgetting her dreams of being hung on the wall from a hook, like a coat, and told to spread her legs. She had gotten an IUD. She had gone on. But she would still carry it, that baby.

Fiona leaves the doll against her stomach, in the car, under her coat. She takes the doll home, carries it now in her arms, like a sleeping kid, up the stairs. She places it at the bottom of the hope chest, beneath her grandmother's linens and the summer bedspreads.

"Good night," she says.

In her dream, it is bright, bright sunlight. She is back at the beach, in Portugal. Her mother and uncle are somewhere, far off, she can't hear their voices. She is walking towards her sister, the sun is warm, diamonds are dancing on the water. Laura is busy making something, kneeling on the sand. She is spelling a word with pebbles, lining up rows of stones to form each letter. Fiona is about to scream, they are golden pebbles, hers, only hers, but the scream dies in her throat. Laura pulls a monster face. Fiona is no longer angry. She gets up suddenly, pulls off her sweater, quickly quickly, daring to show her breasts. They are small and round, they are beautiful breasts. The sisters run along the water's edge, laughing, like real kids. Behind them the pebbles gleam, bright gold in sunlight: *F-I-O-N-A*.

III

HALF OF LIFE

Beira, Portugal, 1936.

He walks towards the house, the late afternoon sun falling on the trees, coolness descending as it always does, evenings, here in Beira. He is sweaty from the day, overdressed with several layers, his silk vest sticking to his shirt, to his undershirt. But he has spent the day in the city, business meetings, one has to dress for such occasions. Here on the farm only a shirt and pants are necessary. The land has appreciated; it is good land, filled with eucalyptus trees. Cork. The farm has done well this year.

He carries in his pocket a hard pink ball, bought from a vendor in Oporto, on impulse. He has never bought her anything before. He walks around the house, avoiding the inside because he wants to see her first, before anyone else. The ball has sagged in his pocket all afternoon, he has grown tired of its weight. He finds her in the corner of the garden, poking a stick at some mud. Spindly legs, feet slightly turned in, the hem of her dress is half undone, from her constant habit of holding it, rubbing it between her fingers. It has never occurred to him to wonder what she does all day, whether she is happy, who she plays with. He hardly gives her a thought at all.

"Leninha," he says.

She turns around quickly, brushes the curls from her face, her mother's black curls, drops the stick in the mud, splattering her ankles. She instantly grabs the hem of her dress as if she needed it for her own survival, like oxygen.

"Your hem," he says.

"I'm sorry, Father," she says.

He pulls out the ball from his pocket, rolls it in his hand, closes his fist on it for a moment.

"I bought this in the city," he says. "I thought you might like it."

She offers up her small hands, arms outstretched, standing carefully at a distance. She could fall over if she bends any farther. He takes a step and places it there, hard and pink, in the small human cup that her hands make. It is as if he has given her a lifetime of happiness in that instant, all condensed into this shiny, pink globe.

She looks up at him, terrified blue eyes, a six-year-old face he has hardly ever scrutinized. A face that doesn't belong to him.

"Oh thank you, Father," she says.

Annibal is not her father, and he knows it.

Helena is sewing when he enters the room, head bent over her fingers, folds of linen across her lap. He is almost surprised to see her, as if her presence were still like an undeserved gift. He has watched her many times, like this, the tiny movements of her hands, the half-closed eyes. Such beautiful hands; he had noticed them first, that day she had walked into his office wearing emeralds at her ears and a black velvet band across her forehead.

"I believe I could be of service to you," she had said. She had phrased it like a question.

She could have asked him for anything, on that day or any other, he would have agreed. He would take her home and live as a happy man, give her his money, his status, all his love. For a while he even believed that she loved him. He could feel her admiration wash over him like a blessing when he walked into a room, introduced himself to her lady friends.

"Here he is," she would say, resting a hand on his arm.

And then he had seen her one day walking alone along the Rossio. She could have been coming from anywhere, but she was smiling. She looked more alive than he had ever thought possible.

He hadn't questioned her that night, as they sat eating silently across from each other. And the following months had passed almost as if he had never witnessed that moment of her exquisite happiness. It was only when they had returned to Beira the following summer that he understood completely. He had come home unexpectedly that day, in the middle of the afternoon, and found two of the towns-women stopped outside the kitchen window, listening. Helena was singing inside, her voice pouring out onto the street, clear as daylight, *gosto de ti, gosto de ti*, she sang, and Annibal had clutched the side of the building for a moment, as if he'd been suddenly ill.

He would not tell her anything. He would watch her body grow heavy with a child that wasn't his, marry her even, for Leninha's sake. He would do it just for the sight of her hands, the way her body moved. At home she walked as though she were infinitely tired. She wrote his letters, sorted his mail, arranged the books in his study. She was useless to him. She was essential.

She tucks in the needle now, at the edge of the fabric. Lifts up her eyes.

"You must be hungry," she says. "I'll call Branca."

"Tell her to bring me some water first," he says. "It was hot like hell up there today."

He makes his way up the stairs towards their room at the far end of the house, the one place where he allows himself to possess her, nights, when the house is silent.

"Let me be, Annibal," she will say.

But he will take his due, all the same. On other days he will feel sorry for her, forgive her almost, and fall asleep listening only to the sounds of her body, breathing beside him.

His shirt has grown cold now, from wetness. He is half-naked and still panting slightly when Branca nudges the door, a large, white jug in her arms.

"Senhor," she says.

The water smells of earth as she pours it into the basin. A sound like something being born.

Coming up behind her he lifts up her skirts. He clutches at her hips.

"Bend over," he says.

At the opposite end of the house, Leninha gets ready for bed. She has eaten her supper alone, as she always does, accompanied only by the clatter of dishes, Branca and Vita gossiping in the kitchen, the odd entreaty from Vita, "Please, *menina*, eat!" Her parents will dine together later, undisturbed. But for bed she is never reluctant, liking the distant quietness of her room, the smooth sheets, the window overlooking the courtyard where a magic tree grows. Every night after Vita has gone, she will walk barefoot across the cool floor and peer out the window, watch the tree that makes oranges and tangerines all at once, fruits dangling in the shadows like jewels. They say her father has made this tree, cut the limbs of one and joined them to another in order to create a tree that bears two fruits, like a rose bush with a different-coloured flower on each stem. She does not understand how this could be so; it must be magic. She knows her father is a powerful man.

"Father gave me a ball today," she says.

"Well, how about that," says Vita. "Senhor Annibal is a generous man, isn't he?"

"Tell me again, Vita, why my father changed your name."

"My name is Vitalina," says the maid, smiling.

"But why do we call you Vita?"

"When I came to this house, Senhor Annibal asked me my name. 'Vitalina,' I said. 'Vitalina?' he said. 'Sounds like Vitamina. We'll have to call you Vita.' And that's how he changed my name."

"Can't I call you Vitalina sometimes?" asks Leninha.

"What you call me matters very little in this world, *menina*."

Vita runs thick fingers through Leninha's curls, bends down to kiss her cheek.

"Sleep well, little duck. Tomorrow I'll let you splash in the water tank."

Alone, Leninha stands at the window, the hard pink ball in her hand. Arm dangling, she spreads open her fingers and feels the weight slip silently from her hand. She runs back to the bed, not waiting to watch it fall.

"Any visitors today?" he asks her. He is working at his plate with deep concentration.

"Of course not," she says. "Who could there be?"

She is safer here, he knows. Away from Lisbon, away from her lover, whoever he is. Or perhaps it is he who is safe.

"I thought your sister was supposed to visit this week," he says. "You are looking rather tired, you know."

"We have a problem."

"Problem?"

"It's Vita. It seems she is pregnant."

He pauses. Takes a moment to finish chewing the meat in his mouth. Swallows the rest of his wine. This one isn't his, of that he's sure. He had stayed away from her because of the girl.

"She will have to get out immediately," he says.

"You don't understand," says his wife. "She has nowhere to go. And Leninha is very fond of her. I can't find a replacement just like that. And there are other circumstances."

"None of that is my concern," he says.

"She was raped, Annibal."

"We'll just have to see about that, won't we."

Helena folds her napkin carefully and stands up. She has seen them more than once, boys and girls of all ages, some of them men already, her husband's illegitimate children scattered all over the countryside. She remembers the boy who had been beaten for stealing a pound of cheese, his scarred face looking up at her with Annibal's eyes. Such old, angry eyes.

"I will not subject this girl to a lifetime of suffering because of what some idiot did to her," she says.

Annibal stands also, walks over to his wife and places both hands around her head. The hot air falls from his mouth onto her face, smelling of wine. He says it almost like a whisper:

"Helena, my love, I will not have more than one bastard in my house."

October now, two months have passed. Annibal comes home early; he is not feeling well. He is never as well here, in the city. Leninha is still in school and Helena is out somewhere, he doesn't care. He is waiting in his study, for something, he doesn't know what. He isn't sorry. All he has ever wanted, what he wanted most, was her.

Branca finds him slumped in his chair. "Mother of God," she says.

The house is full of people by the time Leninha gets home. A smell of softened wax and closed windows. Branca rushes her into the kitchen, pats her gently.

"This is a very sad day, *menina*. I'm sorry to tell you that Senhor Annibal, your father, has died."

And Leninha, who has tossed a pink ball from the window high above the magic tree, runs to her room, not noticing the people in the parlour, or her mother kneeling in the study, with trembling hands. Standing in front of the mirror, Leninha watches her own face and smiles. Days later,

she will fidget on the pavement by her mother's side, waiting for the coffin to be taken away. Branca will rush over
in a panic and say, "Dona Helena, we forgot Senhor Annibal's hat!"

"Have you ever seen a dead man wearing a hat?" her
mother will say. Black dress. Emeralds glinting.

☙

Toronto, Canada, 1991.
Fiona leaves the house early, saying what a beautiful day it is,
and how she feels like a walk. Neil doesn't notice anything;
he sits on the front porch reading the paper, Bea and Zoe
puttering around him.

"Where are you going, Mommy?"

"I'm taking Phoebe for a walk," she says, slipping a collar onto her golden dog's neck.

What she really wants is to be alone, to replay those
three hours in her head. She wants to remember.

The sun is out, the morning cool as she walks by the
playground, up the little hill, the mundane place where
everything has happened. Neil had been asleep the night before when she had walked in. *Be cool,* he'd said. But she was
still shaking. She had slipped into bed, relieved, she didn't
even have to wash. She remembers that feeling from long
ago, waking in a pink bedroom, sticky and sore, thinking, *I
still smell of him.*

She does not recognize them, these sensations. An ache
in her stomach that thrills and hurts her simultaneously, like
the feeling one has in dreams, like falling.

"Why are you doing this?" he kept asking her. "Why are you doing this?"

"I had to have you inside me," she'd said.

And when they had stopped, for a moment, and she was able to find words again, she had asked him the same question. "Why are *you* doing this?

"Because it's Saturday," he'd said.

But he had kissed her with such infinite tenderness, or like a starving animal. She can't even think of it.

Coming up the hill, Fiona sees her. She recognizes the stroller first, dark blue, a purple diaper bag hanging from the side. And then the red hair he'd described. She isn't beautiful. She is walking quickly, the baby fussing in the stroller, three-year-old Emma lagging behind. Phoebe recognizes the baby in the stroller, rushes up to lick the small hands, before Fiona has time to call her back. The woman doesn't stop walking. She looks tired, Fiona thinks. She is rushing home, rushing home to the man Fiona has just slept with. If not for the children, even she would not have known.

This is the beginning, the day after the first time. From now on everything will be different, she will have changed. Or perhaps it is already the middle, because she had decided, seeing him that first time, that she wanted him madly. That she would risk things with almost complete indifference, for this. They had followed each other to the park for weeks, met there, at the same hour, almost every day. She grows desperate when he doesn't appear, like a child wanting a mother who has suddenly vanished, or is late and absent, in the school yard, at the end of the day. And then she spots him walking down the street, towards the park, and her body relaxes, relieved. One day he notices her by the swings, just as he is about to leave.

"I didn't see you," he says.

"I just got here," she says.

"Well, have a good weekend."

But he flashes her the greatest smile, turning, as he closes the gate. A smile of surprise and conspiracy.

And they exchange names, and conversation. They ask each other questions. He takes her for a walk along the beach, a lake that looks somewhat like an ocean.

"Tell me the story of your life," she says.

They each in their own head compare, as the children play between them, sitting on the old quilt he has brought. The children keep them safe.

"I'm surprised I haven't seen you before, around the neighbourhood, I mean," he says.

"We just moved from Montreal a few months ago. My husband doesn't speak French and he was offered a job here."

"I *thought* you looked foreign," he says, smiling.

Fiona prepares to leave. "We should probably be going," she says.

"You're interesting, Fiona. There's a lot that you don't say."

She stares at his hands, giant, beautiful hands he has, because it is easier than looking at his face.

"I find this very scary," she says.

"That's half of life," he says. "Isn't that what they say?"

"What is?"

"Fear," he says.

Walking home, she tells him that she feels like a teenager. He tells her he has been having dreams.

"What happens in your dreams? she asks him.

"Oh, just things."

She looks at his face. She can't quite make out the colour of his eyes.

And so they are lovers. She has become a liar, a dazed actress, putting the Sunlight in the fridge, forgetting the laundry in the dryer.

"Where's your head these days?" asks Neil.

"I'm just tired," she says.

She does not know how to fake it, this wanting, this not wanting. She almost loves her husband more, knowing herself to be shallow. Among other things, what she is guilty of is this: being the first to fall out of love.

"Just don't ever deceive me, Fiona," Neil says.

Bearing down on her, he looks for her face, for the face of a woman he knows. The woman he used to know, who loved him, needed him, who breathed in his jacket before hanging it in the closet. Love me, love me, his body asks. She pulls his head down, pressing it into her neck; she can no longer stand the smell of his mouth.

Days, she is back at the park, trying not to look for her lover with her eyes. This is a small neighbourhood. It is easier when he is not standing next to her; from a distance she can stare. They watch each other through the little green and yellow teepees, miniature worlds that their children play in. They watch each other above the curly heads, thankful for their presence. He is better at this than she is. *Cool*. The summer passes and she is happy, deliriously happy, even though he doesn't tell her much. There isn't a lot of room in his life, he says. This has taken some getting used to: learning to expect nothing. She will even admit having been disappointed after their first night together when he had kissed her quickly and said only, "We'll have to get together again sometime." She calls her girlfriend one night, because she is miserable.

"Just let things go," says Rupa. "Don't become addicted."

"I don't know how he does it," she says. "I can't squeeze myself into compartments."

"Honey, they had it all wrong. There's no such thing as a zipless fuck."

He comes to her one day when the house is empty.

"You are one brash woman," he says.

She isn't sure whether this is sarcasm, in his voice. She thinks she has heard tenderness, at other times, or felt it.

"I never know when I'm going to see you," she says.

"Well," he says. "There will be many nights."

He doesn't give very much with words. Words are traps that he can fall into. Or perhaps she is just presuming. Sex is sex, he'd said, after all. *Because it's Saturday,* he'd said. This is not the answer she had been looking for. But she will take the other stuff, all the same, and be thankful that her milk is sweet.

She wants to ask him if he believes in fate. She wants to ask him what he thinks the purpose of this is. (She turns into a bumbling idiot whenever he is around.) She wants to know what has made him suffer. The sight of him takes her breath away. She wants to know what his greatest wish would be. (Can you ever have a complete wish, after children, after wives and husbands and exes and lost time?) She promises not to ruin his life. (*Many nights, many nights.*)

She believes that it is different, for women. Unfair, he'd said, that he could be inside her body but she could not be in his. Possibly this makes all the difference. When he cracks her open, that's what she likes best. (What she would do to him for a day, for five hours.)

She wants to tell him that he has beautiful children. The thought has occurred to her that he may be a jerk. But she doesn't think so, she doesn't think so. She wants to tell him that he has the most beautiful face she has ever seen. ("There's a difference between a beautiful face and a new, beautiful face," her friend had said. "Honey, suffering will polish you like a diamond.") He has an old, ancient face.

Somewhere in her mind she is waiting for him to fall in love with her. She wants him to go down the list, his list of women, and say that she's the one. The last one. She wants to tell him that she loves him, sing it to him like a mantra, until he understands. *I love you I love you I love you.* Dangerous words. (She won't hold him to anything.) She has no idea who he is. She has seen him write tattoos on his children's arms that say, *I love Mom....* She knows that he likes to turn her over. She cannot see his face, but she is kissing his hands.

The ending can happen in three ways, and she has played each scenario in her head, memorized it like a favourite poem, or parts of a play. An act rehearsed but never meant to be performed, which is nonetheless memorable for what could have been, for the rush of emotion, the applause it would have garnered. In the first scenario she will give up her lover, tell him after a love-making session which has been more poignant for her than for him that it was the last time, that she can't go on being a liar. And he will agree, and feign polite regret even though he is secretly relieved because he felt the affair was intruding on his spare time too much, that she was getting dangerously attached. Or, he could grow serious and intense and finally give her the words that she has craved, knowing how easy it will be to convince her to stay. And she will stay and suffer through her double life until the day she gets careless and her husband finds out, in which case there would be three more ways of ending this, from the husband's point of view.

Or, her lover may agree, and thank her, and resolve to concentrate on his family. They will both behave and try to avoid each other, suffering quietly on their own, and her marriage will dissolve anyway, and she will change and find out that she has always preferred the left-hand side of the bed, where her husband slept. In the interim he will discover that he cannot live without her, that he loves her actually and must be with her at all costs. So he leaves his wife, who is, after some angry suffering, quite understanding of the whole situation, and they make a new life together (assuming, of course, that families can reconfigure themselves without pain), joining their two sets of children, who get along marvellously, and they are happy, happy and at peace. This is her favourite version.

But for now, none of these possibilities exists. Fiona walks to the park with her baby and her dog, cleans house, watches the sun fall on his shoulders as he bends down close over his daughter's head. They chat through the morning, the children nap. She worries that he has tired of her and finds errands to do, thinking that if she makes herself scarce, he will want her more. She doesn't want to live out of his pocket. And then on other days he grows quieter, different, and their eyes meet, and she knows that he wants her again, that he wants to see her. *I'm dying to see you again. I'm dying . . . . I'll jump your bones right now.* And she will live for a time on the anticipation of touching him, feeling his hands on her thighs, pressing down, spreading her apart. With this thought she can go on for days.

But she knows that they are going around in circles, that he will never tell her what she wants to hear. And in truth what really happens is far more tragic, and more banal, than any of the possibilities. But right now she will settle for this, she will take anything. Looking back, she almost wishes they were at the beginning again, days he couldn't keep his eyes off her, when he looked for her everywhere, when they had walked by the edge of the lake with nothing but desire between them. That was their best day, she thinks. When they had walked by the water and he had told her that he had dreams.

IV

SISTERS II (ALBUM)

Snapshot. My grandmother and my great-aunt, waving good-bye. This was the last goodbye, the last moment we ever saw them together. Taken from inside the car, already moving away. They are both smiling, sort of. My grandmother's arm laced into her sister's, leaning. *Lean on me.* My aunt's other arm stretched out, in that gesture that she had, *Heil* Hitler-like. But there is also pain in the faces, a frown between my grandmother's eyes. It is curious, this habit we have, of smiling when we say goodbye. Is it that we want to be remembered this way? We smile for the ones who are leaving. We want them to know that we are strong. We want them to know that we are happy.

In the yellow room, Helena's body lies motionless on the table. She is in the kitchen, where the walls are yellowed with grease, the marble counter tops mottled with stains, worn to a dull polish. The tiled floor is also stained — splattered with blood, that is — from the event that is taking place here. Not a murder or some other gruesome act, but a birth. Helena's daughter's birth.

They have put her in the kitchen for practical reasons. Birth is a messy business, as is death. Both require washing.

The bedding could be spared. The kitchen is warm, also, and the table just the right height for the doctor, who is old and has a bad back. This has been no easy job. They have been at it for twenty hours. Fruitless hours of agony, exertion, frustration. They are all exhausted.

Helena is unconscious now, mercifully, because she would not have survived it, this yanking and pulling. They are all amazed that she has made it this far, in fact. Magdalena stands by her sister's head, holding onto her shoulders, praying for an end.

"Grab her harder, Magdalena. You have to pull." Eusèbio, the doctor, doesn't stand on ceremony. He has known these two sisters since they were girls.

Magdalena places her hands beneath her sister's shoulders and tugs.

"Pull, for God's sake!"

"You're going to kill her!" says Magdalena.

"This baby's going to come out whether she lives or dies, woman. Now shut up and pull!"

Bending down, Magdalena hooks her elbows into her sister's armpits. She presses her chin into Helena's chest. Perhaps some of the pain can be transferred, this way, from one sister to another. Magdalena is strong, she can take it. But she will not look down there, at the other end, where the doctor's hands are groping, entering her sister's body as though it weren't even made of flesh. Somewhere behind the doctor is the midwife, pulling too.

Magdalena clenches her teeth. *Please, God. Not this time.* Pulls.

And then the child slips out, wet and bloody and silent.

Snapshot. My grandmother and sister, a side view. The old lady first, in a dress my mother used to wear, long ago, at the office. First our daughters wear our clothes, then our mothers. Sneakers on her feet. The giant curve of her back, as I always remember it. As a child we would watch her, sitting in the sun, her back exposed to the warmth. *Banhos de sol,* she would call them. Baths of sunlight. Good for the bones. She is leaning on my sister, here, her other hand clutching the purse. Behind her my sister's body, looking so much taller, though she is not tall, it is the grandmother who is little, who has shrunk. Dark, thick hair, on her wrist a round gold band, like my grandmother wears, like my mother. Behind them, the steep incline of old stone steps.

Magdalena lies in the middle of the bed, her sister's daughter wrapped up tightly beside her. She will not sleep, despite her fatigue, the hours of prayer and waiting, the fight. Somewhere in another room Helena will be sleeping, cleaned up, on fresh sheets. But it is Magdalena who is keeping watch: these early hours are critical. And she is mesmerized, anyway, by the tiny network of purple veins covering the eyelids, to which she has pressed her own lips again and again. The velvet head. This transparency is short-lived, she knows; before long the bones close, the tiny body grows opaque, and this daughter will be here, solid and apart.

She will bear her mother's name, Helena, with Maria in front of it. But they will call her Leninha, *little Helena,* from now on. And Maria is a name that Leninha will not care for, later, with its connotations of goodness, and worse, virginity. There is a picture of her, the real Maria, hanging in the dining-room, whose green eyes follow Leninha no matter which end of the room she is in. For the next twenty years this Virgin in her immutable blue dress will seem quite real to Leninha, though not a benevolent presence. An accusatory one. A third mother.

Leninha has been sleeping mostly during these early hours, making the odd bubbly sound. She has opened her eyes only once. No one knows yet whom she will look like. But the eyes are very blue, like Magdalena's eyes. She has taken a bit of goat's milk, from a bottle which Magdalena has prepared. No one expects Helena to nurse. That she has given birth is in itself miraculous. Helena had miscarried five times, before this. Somehow this pregnancy had been different. She had willed it to be so.

Magdalena does not know what has brought her sister's daughter so consciously into this world. She had not been present that night when Helena had sat up in bed for eight hours debating the question, wondering whether or not to abort. A question that is asked, somewhere in a mother's brain, as a prelude to every birth. Nor was she there to see her sister's face that day, as she sat facing the doctor, Eusèbio.

"I don't have to tell you, Helena, that your chances are very slim. We can try, but there are no guarantees. This may take its toll, you know."

"I don't care what I have to do," Helena had said. "I don't care what *you* have to do. Do you understand me, Doctor?"

Eusèbio could swear that he had lived this moment some twenty years before with Helena's mother, Leonor.

"My daughter is not going to die, do you understand me, Doctor? I don't care what it takes, but my daughter is not going to die."

Eusèbio had understood. He had watched Leonor take her daughter into her hands, and heal her by the sheer force of her own will. She would feed her a diet of fourteen eggs a day, and raw meat. Helena would cry merely at the sight of her, walking into the room with a tray full of meat, all rolled into tiny balls.

"All you have to do is swallow, *querida*, just close your eyes and swallow."

"You've created a miracle," he would say, watching the girl grow stronger at each of his visits.

"Don't flatter me, Eusèbio," Leonor would say.

And he would look at her with sad tenderness, knowing that his visits to the house would eventually end. He would have given her much more than flattery, given the chance, though she would never have allowed it. And so it was that he faced it now, this will, replicated in the daughter he wished had been his.

Eusèbio had ordered Helena to spend the last five months of her pregnancy in bed. She willingly obeyed, passing the hours with a needle between her fingertips. She had done this once before in her life, though for different reasons. More was at stake this time than her own survival. In a way she did not mind the seclusion; it kept her away from the trivial, and also from Annibal. There is a kind of retreat that happens in pregnancy, a turning inwards. Her husband would not have understood this, her not wanting to be touched. He seemed to need her more desperately with each passing month, in fact, as if she were slowly being taken from him, for good. He came to her with the silliest of questions, at odd times of the day. He would ask her to fasten his cuff-links. In the early morning, before anyone had waked, Annibal would slip into her bed and grow hard against the small of her back. But now she had the excuse from above, she could come to grips. Nine months was a short time, in the end, for preparation. One had to be ready to receive.

Magdalena had come daily, with books and gossip. She had taken over the running of the house, deciding on menus, dealing with the maids. Annibal's needs had to be attended to, after all. In this way Magdalena would keep her sister company, filling not only the hours but also her own emptiness. Her son, now seven, would fidget in a chair by his mother's side until she could stand the sight of him no longer.

"Go and play, Eduardo, go and entertain yourself."

The boy would stand up, relieved, and kiss his mother and aunt before leaving the room. Magdalena knew that he no longer belonged to her; she could feel the reluctance in his wiry arms during those embraces, embraces which were no longer a child's, and given only on request. Dutiful love.

"He looks more like his father every day," Helena would say.

Magdalena would look away, open the shutters, straighten the bed covers.

Please, don't.

"Is there anything you want? How about some tea? It's extremely stuffy in here, Helena, I don't know how you can stand it. Shall I open a window?"

"Leave it alone, Magdalena."

"Annibal seems a little pale, lately. Has he been working very hard?"

"He's fine. I haven't noticed anything."

"I hope you have a daughter," Magdalena would say.

Snapshot. My great-aunt's face. Short, blond, dyed hair. Dyed until the end. Large gold earrings, but not for pierced ears; snap-ons. Dark brown painted eyebrows. Pearls. A charming smile. This was her happiest birthday, she said. She was ninety. But a smile with the corners of the mouth turned downwards, like those faces my mother used to draw for me when I was little, which meant: sad. You don't see it at first, but there is an arm behind her. A hand resting on her back. My mother's hand.

Magdalena knows that he is back even before opening the door. She can hear him all the way down in the street where she stands, his voice carrying through an open window. Mad, ridiculous piano playing. She climbs up the stairs slowly, legs like lead, breathing hard, as those men used to do who carried bags of coal up the stairs for the stove. In those days the house was always filled with people: her parents, her sister, all the servants, nursemaids, laundresses. And then the people of the street, the vendors and suppliers, who appeared automatically, unbidden but necessary, bringing milk, flowers, meat.

The house has grown emptier over the years, but Magdalena is still here with Maria da Graça and Eduardo. Her parents have left, and Helena too, now living in Annibal's house. She has kept it at least, the house and its rooms full of memories, blessedly empty of him. Empty for good, she had thought.

The piano is so loud here, by the door, even the neighbours must recognize him. Closing it behind her she feels that old dread again, as though for an instant this place were no longer hers. Or hers but taken hostage; occupied. She stares for a moment at Eduardo's room, knowing as she does it that it is useless; she can hear the two of them singing, and Graça's imbecilic laughter.

She comes in on the scene silently, like a voyeur, white-knuckled hand on the doorknob. He is sitting at the piano, of course, a bottle between his knees, with his back to her. It is Eduardo, now twelve, who sees her first. Arms in the air, midway through a pirouette; the boy holds a rose in his mouth. Frozen in the dance he is so gleefully performing for his father. Maria da Graça stops too, bare-legged, her skirt poised in midair.

"Get out," Magdalena says.

Arthur grabs the rose from his son's mouth. "Aren't you even going to say hello, Magdalena?"

"Go to your room, Eduardo, this instant."

"I haven't seen the boy in eight years and you already want him to leave? What have you been doing with him, anyway? He looks like a girl, for Christ's sake."

Maria da Graça gathers up her stockings. "Come along, *menino*."

"You too, Graça, let's all have a party!"

"Leave me alone," says the boy.

"Get out, Arthur. If I have to make you leave I will."

"Tough as ever, eh, Magdalena? He must be rich, who-ever he is, like that old bastard your sister hooked onto. Look, I've only come to get what's mine," he says.

"Nothing here is yours, Arthur."

"Listen, I only need a couple of thousand. Some guys from way back. I thought they'd forgotten, see, but the minute I get back into town——"

The old refrain, again. A song repeated so often that it has lost all meaning.

"No."

Arthur begins to laugh.

"I see. Well, in that case, I'll take what's really mine," he says, gesturing towards the boy.

"You leave him alone!"

"I want to go with Father!"

"You don't have a father, Eduardo."

But then the thought comes to her with sudden clar-ity, displacing all her fear.

"All right, Arthur. Take your son. Take him and get out of my house."

It is Maria da Graça who begins to scream.

"*Menino! Menino!* How could you, Dona Magdalena? You can't let him go!"

Magdalena slaps her maid across the face.

"My son will be back," she says. "He'll be back before the week is out."

Snapshot. My grandmother and sister, again, this time facing the camera. Both have their heads bent, looking down. My grandmother is saying something, something important. *As confidencias.* Their steps match exactly. My sister is holding the chain at her chest. We often do this, clutch at our own jewellery like talismans of safety. My grandmother's finger is pointing, but not at anything in particular. Pointing at the thought, at the point. I watch my own hand, like this, holding poetry books that my grandmother used to read, my crooked index finger pressing down the page. With astonishment I realize it is my grandmother's hand that I am looking at.

In the violet room, Helena opens her eyes. She knows it even before truly waking: something has been taken from her. The weight on her stomach is miraculously gone, yet still somehow there, like an amputated limb that still hurts. Like a memory. Her body, too, remembers, a pain so intense that any aftermath feels like a luxury. Like floating on oily pools of water.

The room comes slowly into focus as Helena turns her head, recognizing the scent bottles on her dresser, a shawl draped on a chair. She stares at these objects vacantly as waves of thought begin to cross her brain. She sees the maids in a flurry of activity, Magdalena rushing in with flushed cheeks. And she sees her own self, as though she were floating high up, in the corner of the ceiling, during all those hours of wanting to climb out of her own body as she clutched her sister's hands.

Help me, she kept saying, *help me.*

There were other words, too, which she can no longer remember: instructions, prayers, pleadings, all a jumble now in these moments of Helena's waking. But she hears them again quite clearly, the two words that flew out of Annibal's mouth: leaving at the outset, he had turned to her and said only, "Good luck."

She doesn't know if he is here now, in the silent house. She has no idea what time or day it is. But she has at least missed it, his return, the first time he set eyes on the child she has made. The thought has not even crossed her mind that the baby may be dead. She knows in the pit of her stomach that her daughter is alive, that somewhere in the house Annibal has seen her, and that she was not there to watch the expression of his eyes at that moment.

Good luck, he had said.

Hearing this, she had known that he, too, would be a keeper of the secret.

She thinks of her lover now, the man who had asked her to keep the baby at all costs.

"This is the most that I can ever give you," he had said. "No one will ever have to know."

And she had wanted it, too, this mixture of their two bodies. Something of his that she could own.

"I'll have to spend the rest of my life with this lie," she had said, knowing as she spoke that she would do it, just for a measure of his face.

Helena sits up now; she wants to see her baby, suddenly, this minute. The pain shoots through her right between the legs, something torn, down there, which hasn't been put back together. I've done it, she thinks, I've survived this. She drags her legs off the edge of the bed and sits facing the nightstand, where a thermometer sits in a glass of water. For the past twenty years Helena has taken her temperature every night, a ritual from the days of her illness when her fever had risen daily, like a tide. The white plague, they had called it. Another name for tuberculosis.

With a smile on her face Helena grabs the thermometer and snaps it in two, the silver beads of mercury running down her bare legs. They hit the floor and scatter, like insects under a bulb.

Snapshot. My mother and great-aunt now, walking. Arm in arm again, though I seldom remember seeing my aunt lean on anyone. Each one is smiling, big-bosomed, and holding a purse. They each walk at the same tempo; one is not slowing down the other. On the ground their shapes make one shadow.

In the white room, Leninha's little body lies on the mosaic floor, a towel beneath her. From this vantage point she can see the curled lip of the porcelain tub, its feet shaped like lion's paws. But she is too dizzy, really, to notice much of anything, having walked already across the long hallway, too tired even to protest. She has a high fever, and they must clean her out, as her mother says. She should be used to these by now; she has had enemas before, one for every fever in her five-year-old life.

"I'm cold, Mother."

"Lie still, Leninha, this will only take a minute."

"You should be doing this in her bed, don't you think? The poor thing is shivering, Helena." It is her aunt Magdalena who says this, walking in.

"There's no need to get the bed all wet and cause more work for everybody," her mother says.

"Poor little thing," her aunt says.

"There you are, Leninha, that didn't kill you, did it?"

Her mother pulls a chain, and the clouded water that has filled her belly gets swirled away.

"Am I all cleaned up now, Mother?"

"For heaven's sake," says her aunt. She scoops the little girl up and carries her to bed, where small square pillows each bear an embroidered *H* on the sham.

"Have you made her a linseed compress?" asks her aunt.

"I don't think it would do her much good," says her mother.

"It may not do much good, but it wouldn't do her any harm, now, would it? That's it, Leninha, you'll feel much better soon. And then Auntie will take you for an outing, would you like that?"

"Don't start, Magdalena."

The two sisters look at each other, each one standing on either side of the narrow bed.

"Shall I read you a story?" says her aunt.

Leninha likes her aunt very much at this moment, but she doesn't know why. Perhaps it is because she is the only person Leninha knows who is not afraid of her mother. Or maybe it is just because she reads her stories. She leans back on the pillows with a sigh.

"Would that be all right, Mother?" she says.

Snapshot. Here they are again, my mother and great-aunt, in close-up. A profile of the two of them, with a stone wall behind. So much of this country is made of stone. Here you see that they have the same face, long and oval, and blue eyes. Eyes that grow more liquid with age. Even my grand-mother's eyes had this blue film on them, in the end. Like the eyes of a newborn, but with blurred edges.

Helena and Magdalena walk down the crowded street, arm in arm, deep in conversation. Their talk is always animated, more like an ongoing argument than a calm discussion. They are totally absorbed in the subject, whatever it is, or in themselves, walking as though encased in a bubble, content and protected.

Leninha stands on the pavement and watches their two shapes advance with amusement. Her mother tall, thin and slower, her aunt short and plump. Hard to imagine one without the other, in these past years. An inseparable pair, like Laurel and Hardy. They come within feet of her, stare blankly at her face, and go on walking.

She is about to call out to them but sucks in air instead, a hand at her mouth. She walks back to the hotel with a smile. They have done without her for so long, a few more hours will hardly matter.

Later, at Magdalena's house, the story brings on peals of laughter.

"Look what we've come to," says Magdalena. "Pathetic!"

"I would have seen her if you hadn't distracted me," says Helena.

"Don't be silly, Helena, you're as blind as a bat."

Helena leans back into a chair, sighs mournfully and says, "Water." Magdalena gets up immediately and disappears into the kitchen.

"You could at least say please, Mother."

"Oh, Leninha, you have no idea how tired I am."

"That's all right, dear," says Magdalena. "She'll be asleep in a few minutes."

"I will not."

"I suggest you take your pill now, before you forget."

"Stop bossing me around, Magdalena. You're always bossing me around."

Magdalena sets the glass of water by her sister's side, covers her legs with a blanket. Within minutes Helena is asleep.

"She always gets cold, you know, by this time of day," whispers Magdalena.

Leninha is amazed, watching this, the marriage be-tween her mother and her aunt. A marriage which has endured beyond all others. Her mother has changed very little, after all; she still manages to be waited on, demand-ing it as though it were her due. She is still thankless. And her aunt, the caregiver, needing both a purpose and a per-son to control. A perfect match.

"She'll never admit it, dear, but she does need a rest every afternoon," says Magdalena. "After all, she *is* getting older."

"She's quite impossible, Auntie, you shouldn't let her talk to you like that."

"Oh, darling, at my age the only great event to look forward to is the funeral, so I might as well make the best of it."

Magdalena laughs, for a moment, contemplating the unfairness of existence.

"You know something, I would rather never have been

born than know that I am going to die." And then, looking at her sister, she says: "Poor thing, I feel sorry for her."

Snapshot. My sister, alone, sneakers on her feet and her hair in a ponytail. She looks young and rested, so unlike the times when I see her, her usual dark-circled eyes. For I have looked into my sister's face recently and seen for the first time the face of an old lady, of the old lady she will become. (Am I comforted, knowing this?) But she is thirty now, looking straight at her husband, who is also young, and standing behind the camera.

And where are the men, you ask, that have so sparsely populated this story? What of Arthur who, tiring of his son after only two days, returned to Angola and shacked up with a prostitute who gave him syphilis? What of Eduardo, the boy, who returned home and said to his mother,"I will never love you"? What of Annibal, the husband, the lover, the men who came after?

There are no men in the photographs. There are no men in this story.

Magdalena wakes in a quiet room. Quiet except for a beeping sound, coming from somewhere. She is not feeling well, not feeling well at all. Someone has stuck a tube into her and left it dangling, up here by her head. Without being told she knows that the beeping is answering her own body, playing it back to itself.

She doesn't remember getting here. Only that they had been walking, she and her sister, along the cafés that line the beach. Heading back to the hotel, she thinks. Helena must be there now, although she doesn't have the room key.

Magdalena has always been in charge of such things. She has always said that they wouldn't go anywhere if she didn't do the planning....

A young woman walks in, dressed in white, with a serious look on her face. At least she doesn't feign cheerfulness, thinks Magdalena. She smells vaguely of vinegar.

"Are you awake, Dona Magdalena? You are at the Hospital Santa Maria, in Ericeira."

It is only while attempting to speak that Magdalena feels the weight on her chest.

"I want my purse," she says. "The key——"

"Don't you worry yourself about that, Dona Magdalena, we will take care of everything. What you need is rest, dear, lots of rest."

"Helena," she says. "She needs the key. You must call Leninha, my niece in Canada. Tell her that I am very sick. Tell her——"

"You'll be just fine," the young woman says.

Magdalena closes her eyes. She will wait for Leninha. Helena, too, is waiting, she thinks, all alone in the room, sequestered. She is thirteen again, and so thin. Magdalena blows her a kiss from the doorway.

"We will be back soon," she says, as her mother pulls her by the hand.

"Come along, Magdalena, your sister needs her rest, and you need some air."

"Can't I stay here," she asks. "Can't I stay with Helena, Mother?"

She hates them, these outings, when Helena is left alone in the room, sitting by an open window. It seems as if she has been ill forever. But Magdalena doesn't mind. All she would like is to keep her company, or read her a story.

"Come along, Magdalena," her mother says.

And she does return, later, from her afternoon by the sea, where she has collected rocks and seashells, saving the prettiest one for her sister. She runs down the street, ahead of her mother, clapping her hands to let Helena know that she is coming, jumping impatiently before the front door until the porter lets her in. She rushes up the stairs, bursting with happiness at the thought of giving her this gift. She opens the door to the room where Helena is still sitting, her bare legs dangling, in a dim triangle by the window.

"Look what I have brought you, Helena," she says.

But instead of a seashell she hands her a baby, whose body is wrapped in white linen, and whose eyes are filled with blue light.

Magdalena opens her eyes once again. Even in death, there is so little time.

"This is it, isn't it?" she says.

Snapshot. My mother and my grandmother, sitting together. They are both facing me, smiling, pale skin over the delicate bones of their cheeks. They are luminous. They are happy. This is the photograph my mother will not be able to bear looking at, later. *Here we are*, they say. *Look*.

V

RAGE

Toronto, Canada, 1993.

When she thinks of him, years from now, Fiona will tell herself that she would never have bought the house if not for the roses.

"I'm waiting for your roses to come out," he'd said, that first spring, calling out from his porch. He would spend the better part of most days there, rocking himself, watching the neighbours come and go.

"If I didn't have a porch I couldn't spy on anyone," he would say, laughing.

He called himself Dusty; a skinny-armed man, hair like straw, still freckled. She had never asked him what his real name was.

Dusty's house stood directly across from hers, a narrow Victorian on a tree-lined street in the east end of the city. Fiona had chosen the neighbourhood for the exuberance of its front gardens in the summer, and because she could walk to the edge of the lake on Sunday mornings, before the crowds got there. It had been her own dog, Phoebe, who had run to him during those first days in the house, as though she'd come back to a familiar place, a place she'd been kept from too long. He would pat her flank silently, or else cock his head to one side and whisper something barely audible, a message she understood implicitly; Dusty and Phoebe communicated with an understanding seldom found between two humans. They were both old.

"You are one bright animal," he would say, "aren't you, girl?"

"You sure you two haven't met in another life, Dusty? You should be careful, you know, she's a sucker for compliments."

"Like I said, a very bright animal."

Fiona would smile, and Dusty would lean forward on his elbows, widen his eyes and lower his voice, which meant that he was about to say something important.

"Animals are just like people, Fiona. Some are smart, and some are dumb. Take my daughter, for instance. Hasn't done a single intelligent thing in her whole life."

"Come on, Dusty."

"You don't believe me, do ya? Did you know that I offered her this house? No sir, little miss rich bitch had to go up and live in Thornhill, with that wimpy husband of hers. Never spoke to me again."

"That's too bad, Dusty."

"Well, it's not hurting me, but it's hurting her."

Everyone gets hurt, Fiona thought.

After a time she would cross the street and enter her own house, sometimes leaving Phoebe on the porch with the old man. She knew the dog would be safe, lying there in the shade. And closing the door she felt safer, too, with Dusty's eyes on the red roses that climbed up her walls. Sitting in the apple-green kitchen Fiona sorts through her mail. She had always told herself that when she had her own house, a house that had no memory of Neil in it, she would have an apple-green room. And she likes it now — *it makes everything look green, Mom, it hurts my eyes!* — though it never approximates in beauty the places she invented, rooms she would slip into when his moods came in on her like waves, like a mean sea.

"I'm in a funk," he used to say.

Neil was an actor in search of a Spanish villa.

Fiona would stare blankly at him, or rest her back against his chest. This way she didn't have to look at his face. But in her head she was already in some other place, a yellow room that was always light filled, with a circular bay of windows in it and the sounds of a garden, coming from somewhere. Or in a square room made of thick, white walls where she was kneeling, naked, in the centre of a red stone floor, giving thanks for she knew not what.

But this was a later escape; earlier on she would have thought intently and struggled for a solution, navigated his rejections carefully and cheered on the hopeful auditions where every gesture, smile or raised eyebrow had a meaning.

"I thought your audition went well," she would offer.

"You just don't get it, Fiona. I'll never get anywhere as long as I stay in Canada. The whole system is different there. They treat you like a person. If I went back to L.A. I *know* I would get work."

Fiona tried to listen carefully. She noticed he said *I* instead of *we*.

"We can't just pick up and leave, again, Neil. We can't afford it."

"Sometimes you have to be willing to struggle for

things, Fiona. You have to take chances. Do you understand what I'm saying to you?"

L.A. She remembers now. The great city, full of pretty people. An unending grey landscape; even from the air you couldn't see its edges. The ugliest place she had ever seen. But he was pretty too, then, and so convinced that he would get his share of the adoration.

"This is a crazy town," he'd said, picking her up at the airport.

She wondered why he used the word *town*. He had called smaller Montreal *city*. He sounded different, like those times she heard him on the phone, talking to some casting agent. He sounded alive, and far away from her. You could really belong to a town, she supposed. Become part of the scenery, like the opulent flowers that seemed to grow everywhere, the gleaming lawns, the empty paint cans piled in corners of parking lots.

They had sublet an apartment in a quiet spot, from some actress who had left for a shoot. And Fiona had brought her dog, and a set of sheets, which she had ironed. And he bought her a rose, and cooked a disastrous salmon, which went down in history, in *their* history, that is, as a very funny episode. He showed her the Pacific, which was very blue, and stretched along ribbons of highway as if by accident; as if the highway had been there first. He showed her all the neat places, pockets of beauty and money, and she was almost convinced. She wanted so much to believe in this dream of his.

When he went for an audition, Neil came back humming.

"How did it go?"

"The director really liked it. He gave me a really nice handshake at the end. What a wonderful man. He said 'I'm sure we'll be seeing you very soon.' "

Neil did not describe the director, saying these words. He acted him, complete with handshake and facial expressions.

"Oh," said Fiona. "Do you think you'll get it?"

"Well, there aren't many actors like me around."

"L.A. is full of actors, Neil."

"Pretty faces, you mean. It's rare to find somebody real."

"Oh." And then: "It would be great if you got it, darling."

Neil got very horny when he was happy.

"I think he really liked it," he'd say.

Next door, Lassie's chains are rattling. She hears it again, the raspy breathing, and soon after, the high-pitched sob. The dog must be choking. Fiona looks out front, but the drive is empty. She walks out along the side of the house, down the narrow passage overrun with weeds, towards the backyards. Stretching out her arms she can touch her own house and theirs, the buildings are so close here, in the city.

The boxer has tangled itself up in its chain, which they've tied to the metal stairs leading down from the porch. He must have gone up and down or through something, she doesn't know. But his head is stuck close to the edge of the stair, leaving him almost suspended there; he can barely breathe. Fiona steps lightly: dog shit everywhere.

"OK, Lassie. Easy boy, down."

The dog is trying desperately to jump up, his cropped tail shaking frantically, he is so happy. He steps over and over

into his own excrement. The chain around his neck is so
tight it bruises her fingers to unhook it. She frees him,
finally, but can't let go of the collar: Lassie goes completely
wild when let loose.

Moi j'aime beaucoup Lassie, the woman had said.

Lassie jumps up now, getting Fiona's shirt all dirty,
scraping her leg with his paw.

"Fuck," she says.

The dog is so strong she can barely hang on. A thing of
beauty, really. Deep golden brown, with dark stripes along
his rib cage, *comme un tigre*, they had said. A hopeless face.

Now what? She cannot hang onto him and untangle
the chain at the same time.

"There you go again, snooping in other people's yards.
I'll have to turn you in one of these days, Fiona."

Dusty. Thank God.

"Can you imagine giving a male boxer a name like
Lassie, Dusty?"

"Stupid idiots. Poor thing would be better off dead."

Fiona stands very still for a moment, struck by a sudden thought. She watches Dusty unravel the chain and tie
it to a fence post near the tree. He fills a grungy bowl with
water.

"Why do they do this, Dusty? They're not bad people,
you know. Why would they want a dog anyway?"

"They don't want a dog," he says. "They just want to
own something."

Fiona puts on some music. *Crummy sound*, Neil had said,
looking over her new house. Maybe. But *hers,* and enough to

drown out Lassie, who still cries by the fence, out of loneliness. At least he didn't want custody of the dog, she thinks, watching Phoebe by the door.

She is still unaccustomed to it, the silence. Or the absence of — *what?* — her children, in the beginning: watching them leave with their knapsacks.

See you later, alligator.

Bye-bye, Mommy.

But something more than that. *Freedom from Fear*, that's what he'd called it, the Norman Rockwell painting of a man and woman tucking their children in for the night. A perfect family. Everyone safe. Or perhaps the title belonged to another painting, a portrait of several people, heads bent in prayer? She doesn't remember.

"Mommy and Daddy are going to live in separate houses," she had explained.

"Are you getting divorced?" Bea had asked.

And afterwards, months of screams and threats, explanations, attempts at reason, affidavits flying back and forth like darts.

I'm going to fight you for the kids.

"Please don't do this," she'd said. "If you do this you will destroy everything." This was the only time she would beg him for something, ever.

You fucked someone else and I'm the one who's destroying, right? I gave you my life, Fiona.

But they had lived through it, in the end, passing the days with a semblance of normality, shopping for groceries, mowing the lawn. She remembers less of it now, except her daughters' pain, moments of terror she cannot erase.

"When Daddy be home?" Zoe had asked.

She is only two, Fiona had thought, she will not remember.

But Beatrice would. Fiona had sat in the community centre gym, one morning, waiting for the Spring Showcase to begin. Nothing had prepared her for the sight of Bea, five years old, wearing a tutu with pink and yellow paper petals around her face, dancing in her first ballet. There must have been two hundred parents, all there for the same reason. Fiona had wanted to jump up and down at the sight of her, a little girl searching the sea of faces for her face, for the eyes that said *Yes, I'm here, I'm watching only you. Dance for me.* Thin, delicate arms, pointed toes, round belly.

Tomorrow, my love, I will give you a happy day. I will give you anything, anything to make you happy. There should be joy, in a house where little girls live.

Joy. She could hardly remember what it felt like.

Here's what she can't stand about him:

The way he closes the juice bottles, so tightly, no one can open them.

The way he stirs his yoghurt.

The shape of his calves, slightly bow-legged, like his father's.

How he walks downstairs every night after the children are in bed, and pours himself a glass of milk.

I can't stand his breath on me, Mom.

Good heavens.

She hates him for these things. *Hates him.* Can you believe it?

Everyone has an opinion, and she tells the story over and over, to old and new friends.

"Somewhere, in the back of my mind, I always knew I was the one who —— the one —— "

"Spit it out, Fiona."

"I was the one who loved less, Rupa."

"You know, some people have an affair, talk about it for three months, and forget it," says Rupa. "I think that's a good policy, don't you?"

"He's not a bad guy, Rupa, I know he is a *good* man. . . . He had warm hands —— "

"Honey, Jake was a good guy, too. That's why he got on my nerves."

Fiona hears the car in the drive. She waits a few moments before stepping out again; there are always parcels to be removed, discussions, before her neighbours make it into their house.

"Mme. Laluz?"

"Fiona! How are you, *chérie?*"

Mme. Laluz always speaks as though she were on the verge of a huge embrace.

"Fine, thanks. I just wanted to tell you — Lassie — was choking with his chain."

"Lassie?"

"Yes." Fiona uses her hands, pretends to choke.

"Oh, no!"

"It's all right. I moved him. I put him by the fence. It's too dangerous on the stairs." And then she repeats it, to make sure they understand: "The stairs. Too dangerous for Lassie."

"Ah! Yes."

Meanwhile, Mr. Laluz has brought Lassie to the front of the house.

"Bad dog!" yells Mme. Laluz. She takes the leash and holds it above the dog's head, poised as though she is about to strike. The dog sits and cowers, his whole body trembling, caught between terror and joy.

"Sit," she commands. "You see how well he listen?"

"Lassie is a good dog," Fiona says.

"We see you, *chérie*. And thanks!"

They are about to enter the house.

"Mme. Laluz? Can I take him for walks, sometimes, in the school yard or the park?"

"Ah! Sure. Anytime."

"Thank you," she says.

It was the Christmas before Zoe was born. She had been dressing for a party that night. She wore a white satin blouse, lacy camisole underneath. Loose enough that her belly, still only the size of a small melon, would not show.

"A bit much, don't you think?" he said.

"No. Why?"

"It's a dinner, Fiona. You know how they are. They don't get all dressed up just for a dinner."

"It's Christmas," she said.

"You'll look like a fool," he said.

Fiona swallowed. She had thought that it would lessen with the pregnancy, his scrutiny of the way she looked. A thing she had liked, in the beginning, confusing jealousy with desire.

You're beautiful, he had told her that first day. They had been walking in the cemetery, behind the old school buildings on St-Croix. They had stopped under a row of poplars and listened to the sounds of a trumpet, a song coming from an open window somewhere.

You're so beautiful.

She had tasted his lips, then, and placed her hand on the inside of his arm, where the skin was white and smooth. For a moment she had thought that love must be like dying: a surrender to the inevitable, a giving in to light.

"I'm pregnant," she said now. "No one will look at me."

Neil pulled her to the bed. He began to lean over her, pressing on her shoulders with his hands. He had done this at other times, during arguments, leaned over with his weight on her, addressing her as though she were an adolescent while trying to make her laugh. She remembered that discussion, regarding a man who had killed his wife after seeing her at a restaurant with someone else.

"Understandable rage," Neil had said.

"For sitting at a restaurant? Why would he assume she was having an affair, anyway? Would you kill someone over that?"

"You don't understand," Neil had said. "He doesn't want someone else's prick in her."

He doesn't want someone else's prick in her. This is a phrase she would remember.

Neil unbuttoned Fiona's blouse.

"I'm looking at you," he said.

There is something in a man that doesn't want his wife to be too pretty, Fiona thought.

"Stop it," she said.

"Says who?"

Fiona was naked. He slipped into her, carefully at first, because of the baby. Stared suddenly at her face as though she were about to vanish.

"Fiona," he said.

But she had already crawled out from under him, and run into the other room, a room she had painstakingly decorated, before Beatrice had been born, with flowered curtains and wallpaper. She sat on the rocking-chair, staring at the pristine change table that she and Bea had stocked already with diapers and baby wipes, in readiness for the next child. A second child whose round face would make up for an unutterable loss, years before. She clutched her knees up to her chest, pressing the tight ball in her stomach into her back. Sobbing.

Neil stood above her, hands limp at his sides.

"Will you please tell me what I did wrong. Please?"

She could not speak.

"Come on, Fiona, come on...."

In this moment he was almost more helpless than she.

Fiona tends her roses at the front of the house. They are blood red, with a deep, warm scent. She does not know who planted them, but the bush is very old; she has had to remove several wooded canes. And she has learned where to make the cut, on each stem, so that the bush will bloom again.

Across the street Dusty is chatting with his lady friend. Fiona has seen her more often recently, a curly-haired, overweight woman who walks with a limp. Her name is Lynette. Fiona hears them laughing, and thinks hopeful thoughts.

"Come on over and join us," yells Dusty.

She places a few roses in a glass of water and crosses the street, Phoebe panting with delight.

"There you are, sit yourself down a while."

"It's nice to hear you two laughing," Fiona says.

"I'm just trying to get this woman to come and live with me, and she's giving me a hard time. Wants to change things around and she hasn't even moved in yet!"

Lynette laughs and shuffles her feet.

"I said to him I'm not moving in here unless he gets a TV. With cable."

"Miss TV, that's who she is."

"Well, Dusty, you can't expect to provide all the entertainment, can you?" Fiona says.

The old man slaps his thigh and looks astonished. "Damn it, Fiona, I think you're right. So you think I should get a TV, do ya?"

"Absolutely."

"You girls are all the same," he says. "My daughter wouldn't take her eyes off the thing if the house was burning down. You know, I gotta get me one of those boys with a big mouth and a strong back to dig up my garden for me. I'M GETTING OLD, YOU KNOW."

"You *are* old," says Lynette. "Can I get you a piece of pie, dear?"

"No, thanks. But I think it's wonderful that you two are going to live together."

"We'll live in sin," laughs Dusty.

"How long were you married, Dusty?"

"Thirty-seven years," he says. "She's buried over there in Mount Pleasant. I've got my space next to her, but I don't care. She can't bother me if I'm dead."

"You're terrible, Dusty."

"You think I'm joking, don't ya?"

There were moments of happiness also. Days filled with the children, the house, the business of living. Trips they took, the car piled high with suitcases and baby gear, markers and colouring books strewn across the floor. A rainy day in Stowe, where they walked along paths with orange plastic ponchos covering their bodies and heads, Phoebe running along ahead, tongue hanging, wet and happy, all of them. They stopped by a brook with a small bridge, a place that held magic for their daughters, like the giant mushrooms that grew under trees. They blew bubbles on a drenched tennis court surrounded by woods, bubbles sticking to the pavement, the net, the flowers, none of them bursting.

They had watched their children running, in meadows, in parks, on the hard-packed snow of fields where they pretended to spot a bear.

They had collapsed into bed after runny noses and fevers and found things to laugh about, or made love when they were too tired for words.

Of course, she could tell herself that the children eclipsed everything, that so much happiness was spent on them. She could barely see him, at times, across the dinner table. She missed him even when she was with him.

And other days, when she felt parcelled out, *a piece for you, and you, and you,* when her daughter looked up to her with such needy expectation, to meet only the blank stare of an exhausted mother. Pockets of deadness falling across her face like shadows.

"I think Mommy's tired, Bea," Neil would say.

"Yep. She has no batteries. What are we going to do with this boobie gal?"

Songs that always brought her back to life.

At what point does she stop being a part of him? When does the line get crossed that tells her she is on the other side, and can never go back? She notices that his chin is starting to hang, and is unmoved.

Ultimately, we are what we came from. Fiona knows this, watching him with his family.

"Don't ruin my Christmas," he says.

"I don't understand you," she says.

He feels assaulted.

They forget how to be kind to each other. They love their children. He sulks when they do not have sex.

"I want my life back," he says.

His life?

Maybe she only thought she was a part of him. Maybe she never was.

He places his hand on her face, one night after they have already been sleeping apart, leaning over Bea who has taken his place in the bed, her silent and curious eyes upon them. She holds onto his arm, holds his fingers there, for a few seconds. He is worried about some test she has had, know-ing there might be a chance of something grave.

Or is it that he feels sorry for her? She thinks that per-haps he loves her still. She feels it in his fingers, leaving that hot imprint on her face. She remembers it, that warmth, the heat his body always gave her. How it stilled her.

She tries to create her own heat now, with hot-water bottles at her feet and her daughters' bodies next to her. They put her to sleep, feeling safer, as she does. But it is not the same.

She wants to crawl into his bed this night, put her back against his belly, hoping that if he is half asleep he will not fight it, this remembrance. But fear holds her back. They do not want to confuse the issues, do they? The battle looks clearer between definite enemies. For this is what they do now: battle over territory.

In the end, all wars are the same.

She wants to beg his forgiveness, tell him she still wants him, despite the moments of hate. Make him under-stand her need to be separate. It might even be easy to lock into each other's bodies again, to wake in the morn-ing, but she knows that the pieces wouldn't fit, eventu-ally.... And if they did, how to erase the things they've said, the horrible acts of war, all the allegiances they have reorganized?

In light of all this he seems quite insignificant, her lover; the least of her worries.

None of this gets said. They will go on ruining each other, forgetting who they were when they laughed, made babies and planted apricot trees.

Dusty repairs the house. He keeps a supply of tools and materials in the shed out back, scraps he has collected, mostly. But for this he has been extravagant: bought a new vanity and mirror for the bathroom, with a set of lights along the top like they have in the dressing-rooms, she will like that. He has even replaced the naked bulb on the ceiling with a small fixture, a pinkish globe that was on sale.

He rarely ventures into the bathroom these days, except when necessary. But Lynette will be different: she won't have the face staring at her, a disembodied head, floating, open-mouthed, in the grey tub. For this is how he found her, his wife: angry even in death. Yellow hair floating around her head like tentacles, a washed-out Medusa.

"This house will be the end of me," she would say, staring out the window. "Will you get me a blanket? I'm freezing in this place."

Towards the end she could only ask for things, which secretly thrilled him. He could choose to ignore her pale-green stare, her dry hands.

Most ironic of all was her name: Gladys. A woman who had chosen to be miserable all her life.

"You have to make it easier for her, Dad, you have to make the house more accessible," his daughter had said.

"More what?"

"She could fall and break her hip or something, don't you understand?"

"She's not going anywhere," he'd said.

It was after Gladys died that his daughter changed, putting on her mother's face like a mask.

"I'll never forgive you," she said.

Dusty presses the button slowly; he is drilling through tile, which is tricky. But the bit hits something hard, suddenly a piece of tile goes flying and hits him in the head, right above the eye.

Dusty is bleeding. He leans over the new cabinet with its gleaming white sink and watches the blood drip into the bowl, a trail of red veins like the centre of a flower.

"Damn you," he says.

Fiona goes to Lassie again. She cannot stand it anymore: he has been whimpering all morning.

"Come on, Lassie, we're going for a walk."

She has brought Phoebe's leash and holds on tight, with Lassie jumping and pulling in every direction. They drag each other, this way, to a fenced-in school yard where she can let him go, and watch.

Lassie takes off as though ignited, running, leaping, circling the huge field with insane happiness. He twists and turns, flips in midair, drags his nose through the grass and throws up mounds of dirt with his paws. Every few seconds he comes back to her and brushes by, or knocks his body against her legs.

"Hey!" she says.

Fiona claps her hands as tears of rage fall down her face, laughs, and cries out his name.

"Hello, Fiona, where are the little ladies today?"

"With their father," she says. "Daddy day."

"What are you doing with yourself?"

"I took Lassie for a walk today. You should have seen

him, Dusty. I think he would have run until he lost consciousness."

Dusty shakes his head.

"Do you think he will ever get used to it, the loneliness, I mean?"

"Well, we all have to be alone, sooner or later. You know something, it just occurred to me the other day: I can't buy any more green bananas."

Fiona doesn't get it. "Why not?"

"I don't know if I'm gonna live long enough to eat them! Ha! Ha!"

Fiona's daughters are in bed. They sleep on clean sheets, bodies still damp from a warm bath, after kisses and stories, Mother Goose rhymes.

> *Peter, Peter, Pumpkin Eater,*
> *Had a wife and couldn't keep her.*
> *He put her in a pumpkin shell,*
> *And there he kept her very well.*

Phoebe is also snoring in her spot by the stairs. Fiona bends down and breathes in the scent of her paws, which smell of heat and fur and grass and earth — the smell of peace.

Outside, the rain begins to fall. A cool rain, announcing the end of summer. She does not know it yet, and she will prefer not to think it a coincidence, but in the spring following Dusty's death, Fiona's roses will fail to bloom.

She steps outside, a plastic bag in her hand, garden

shears in the other. She has done her bit of research, looked into aspirins and sleeping-pills, even antifreeze fluid, all supposedly deadly. But she has chosen the simplest, in the end. They have gone out again; no one will know.

"Oh Lassie, look what I have for you."

She pulls the chocolate out of the bag, bars and bars of it, and lets him eat. He is still long enough to let her pat his head. In a few hours, his heart will stop.

"Good boy," she whispers. "Lassie is such a good boy."

Out front, Dusty and Lynette rock together, and the rain falls on the street like a blessing.

VI

RICE

Montreal, Canada, 1986.

You would never know it, looking at the table, that she hates to cook. The meal spreads out across the white tablecloth, lush, moist platters, the best breads, colour. Leninha never makes too much; just the right quantities, leaving you satisfied, but with the possibility of having had more. Tonight she made a snapper: red as a jewel it was and clear-eyed, with small potatoes roasted in herbs, puréed broccoli mounded like ice-cream atop cooked carrots, and, of course, the rice, her specialty, golden brown and tossed with snow peas. What's more, the kitchen is spotless, as if no one had worked here, all the pots cleaned and put away. And in the centre of the table, always, a ring of flowers cut from her garden that morning.

Helena and Magdalena, Leninha's mother and her aunt, have been in Canada for two weeks now, a trip Magdalena had meticulously planned months ahead of time. Leninha has taken them to all the expected places, the churches and museums, the shopping malls with their huge, interior worlds. And she has fed them, of course, three times a day.

The old ladies sit at the table now like children at a

party, hungry and eager, but not innocent; greedy. They have already attacked the bread, which they butter on both sides, and dug into platters before she has even sat down. Fiona and Joaquim have the grace to wait, knowing better.

"Goodness, Mother, you two look as if you haven't eaten in days," Leninha says.

Under the skin of her pale cheeks she feels the heat rising, but sends it back down with a gulp of wine. She is amazed at it, the lack of manners that seems to appear with old age, like accompanying body smells, rot. Or perhaps only with these two, she thinks.

Fiona places her hand on Leninha's shoulder. "It looks beautiful, Mom," she says.

She has been watching Leninha's irritation mount all afternoon, like a volcano ready to erupt at any minute. Fiona is the only one who knows how to help her mother in the kitchen without getting in the way. One has to be fast, because Leninha always cooks as if she were in a terrible rush and had ten important businessmen waiting with her husband in the next room, about to clinch a deal whose outcome depended on the quality of the food she prepared.

Fiona remembers them, of course, the real business people who came to the house throughout her girlhood and sat in the living-room with her father, Joaquim, sipping martinis and holding peanuts in their hands. She grew up watching her father stride to the dining-room table as if he were the creator of all its splendours, or had summoned them by magic. Her mother would then pull off her apron and pull on the conversational smile she had mastered so well, as if they meant nothing, her hours of suffering in the kitchen. It was always the guests who offered her thanks, and compliments, though it seemed to Fiona that even these somehow reverted back to her father, whose many qualities included the possession of such a charming and talented wife.

Fiona had asked her mother, once, when she and Laura were old enough to become part of the kitchen crew, why she stood for it.

"Why does it always have to be you? Why don't you tell him?"

Leninha had paused, watching the water in a pot of rice boil over for a moment before lifting the lid and blowing, quickly, on the rising white steam.

"You don't understand, Fiona," she said. "Mind your own business."

Helena, Leninha's mother, lifts up her plate now with both hands and peers minutely at her food, being myopic. "Let me see," she says, peering at the little green and orange trees that surround her dish like a miniature forest. "Ah. Broccoli. How interesting," she approves.

"You know, Leninha, cousin Amelia used to cook this way," says Magdalena. "Every plate was a picture, poor thing."

"Why do you say poor, Auntie?"

"Well, she suffered very much with her husband, you know. He was a mean man."

"A horrible creature," says Helena.

"You see how lucky you are?" says Joaquim, smiling at Leninha.

"Is there more bread?" asks Helena, staring at a basketful right in front of her.

She's not that blind, thinks Leninha. But she answers,

instead, to her husband's sweet gaze: "You are an angel, my love, yes you are."

"Sometimes," says Fiona.

"Is that so, young lady?"

Magdalena. who is still following the path of her own thoughts, sighs between bites and continues: "And she died, of course. She died long ago."

The insects hide in the flowerpots, or under them. Leninha knows this, having watched the turtle snap them, quick, with a stretch of the neck. She doesn't remember whether they fed him anything else, but perhaps her mother did. She used to watch him for hours crawling along that big veranda where he lived, filled as it was with plants and flowers, or else swimming in the long, clay trough whose sides were slippery and green. When she picked him up with both hands he performed the most amazing disappearing act. She would have liked to feel his feet flapping against her palms, just once, as they did in water.

From the veranda, which looks out onto the back terrace, she can see Nuno and Sem, two dark heads partially obscured by the sheets hanging on the line, giant squares of white linen swaying in the air like sails. It is Nuno she is looking at. He lives on the ground floor of the apartment building, and Leninha loves him more than any other being on earth. She even prefers his flat to her own because it has toys in every room, and an electric train set, a real train, Nuno calls it, that makes smoke and whistles. Nuno's father is a scientist, a small man with very little hair whose hands always look as if they are covered in white chalk. Leninha likes his mother more because she gives them candies, small chocolates shaped like umbrellas, and calls her *querida*.

Sem lives on the top floor, but Leninha doesn't go to his house very often. Sem's father must be a teacher of some kind because everyone, even Leninha's mother, calls him the Professor. Sem's house is filled with books: they line the shelves on walls and are piled up in the most unlikely places. Leninha used to think that Sem's mother must be very sad because her own mother always says she is poor when she talks about her.

"Poor Dona Maria. What sorrow!"

Leninha has only recently begun to realize that her mother talks this way because Sem is retarded. This also explains why a ten-year-old boy would spend so much time playing with Leninha and Nuno, who are only six. Sem likes to follow whatever Leninha and Nuno are doing, and usually obeys their commands. Sometimes he gets angry, for no apparent reason, and rocks his body back and forth, or stomps his feet, and cries.

"I don't want to," he says. "No I don't want to."

When Sem cries his tongue sticks out more than usual and his eyes, which are very pale and round, darken. Leninha doesn't like to look at him then.

She leans over the railing. "I've got some, Nuno!"

"Hurry up!" he says.

Leninha runs back down the stairs and into Nuno's house, then through his kitchen and onto the terrace. In her hand is a small glass jar taken from Nuno's father's study, filled with bugs.

"Just what we need for the soup," says Nuno.

"Soup," says Sem.

On the floor in front of them, resting between Nuno's knees, is a small stone bowl. This bowl and the pestle that goes with it are Leninha's contribution, apart from the bugs, confiscated from the kitchen in a moment when Branca the maid wasn't there. What Leninha likes most about this bowl is its thickness and its weight, which make it seem precious, like an ancient relic. When the pestle hits the sides of the bowl it makes the sound of marbles rolling on stone.

"I've got tons," she says softly, speaking only to Nuno.

Sem bends over the bowl and asks, "Is it ready?"

"Push over," Nuno says. "I can't see anything."

Sem gets up and begins to walk around the terrace as though he were looking for something. When he walks under the clothes-line, a piece of sheet brushes by his face and over his head. He stretches up his arms, smiling, and lets the white cloth brush over him again and again, swaying, slowly, back and forth, over and over, soft and cool as a cloud.

"Look," he whispers. "Look!"

But Leninha and Nuno are too busy crushing bugs into the bowl, one by one. A mixture of water, stones and dirt, darkened now with the crushed bodies of insects and some soap, for bubbles.

"It's ready," Leninha says. "Hey, Sem, come and have some soup!"

But Sem is enveloped in his own happy silence.

"Come on!" says Nuno.

The boy walks over, dull, as if he had just been awoken from sleep.

"It's really good," Nuno says. "We tasted it."

"I want some too."

Leninha's heart beats faster as she watches him lift up the pestle.

"This is not a spoon," he says.

"We'll get one," Nuno says. "Just start sipping."

Nuno runs into the house pulling Leninha by the hand, and slams the door closed behind them as if they were escaping a terrible but thrilling danger. Leninha brings her hands to her mouth and giggles. Soon she is laughing so hard that she has to bend over.

On the terrace, Sem sits down with the bowl and stirs for a while before bringing it to his lips.

"Thank you," he says, remembering.

It is almost dark that day when Leninha's mother gets home. Or she may have been home for hours before finding out. But Leninha knows from Branca, whose face is redder than usual and has tiny beads of sweat along the upper lip, that something is wrong.

"You are to come upstairs right away, *menina*," she says.

Leninha's mother's eyes are dark and glassy, as though she has a fever. She holds in her hand the pestle, still dirty from the soup that Leninha and Nuno have already forgotten. Leninha has never heard her mother's voice, which is usually low and deep, go so shrill and loud.

"Will you tell me the meaning of this? Will you, Leninha? Do you realize that Sem could have been seriously ill?"

She slaps her daughter across the face, leaving on her cheek the red imprint of her hand. Leninha feels the heat rise to her face like a wave of shame, permanently displayed there for all the world to see.

"You think you are very smart, don't you? This is the last time, do you understand me? I told you I couldn't stand that boy. You are never to play with Nuno again. Never. You want to make soup, do you? I'll put you in the kitchen with the maids, daughter, that's what you'll do."

This time it is her mother pulling her by the hand, across the corridor and into the kitchen. Crossing the marble threshold Leninha stumbles, her free arm flying across a table near the door. In the frenzy, a jar of rice gets knocked over and spills onto the floor.

"Now look what you've done."

Leninha drops to her knees before her mother's body without being asked and holds up her hands as though she were about to pray. She has performed this gesture many times before, though more often in front of her father.

"I beg your pardon, Mother, please forgive me."

On the floor, the grains of rice dig into Leninha's knees, leaving deep red dents like the wrinkles of sleep. They hurt her as if she were kneeling on broken glass, as if the jar that had contained them had also crashed, and she had kneeled on it, unthinking, begging for forgiveness.

They all sit in the den after dinner, watching television. Helena closes her eyes almost immediately, resting her head back, immobile, with a faint trace of lipstick still on her lips. Watching her, Leninha thinks that her mother will never look like an old lady, possessing as she does this beautiful, arrogant face, even in sleep.

Magdalena, on the other hand, has already changed into her slippers and bathrobe, her skin glossy from a fresh application of night cream. She is sewing a new set of buttons on one of Fiona's blouses as she watches the television, one of her legs swinging all the while, to and fro, like a pendulum.

"Who is this one?" she keeps asking. Sometimes she answers herself, out loud: "Ah, he's married to the blond one. Now I'm getting it."

Joaquim sits in his chair and picks at a piece of food caught between his teeth, making little noises that alternate between sucking and kissing.

"Please, Joaquim!" Leninha snaps.

"Are you nervous, Lena?"

"No, I'm not nervous. Can you get that thing out of your tooth?"

"I thought you seemed a little nervous."

"Do you think I could watch five minutes of this show?"

"Jesus," he says.

"What's going to happen next, Leninha?" Magdalena asks.

Leninha breathes out and answers, resigned, like an exhausted mother whose child has been asking too many questions.

"I don't know, Auntie, I couldn't hear anything."

She crosses her legs and wiggles her foot, side to side, in a tempo that is twice as fast as her aunt's.

Fiona stands up and prepares to leave. "Thanks for the buttons, Auntie. Dinner was great, Mom."

Leninha looks up at Fiona with eyes that are almost pleading. *Don't leave me here, please.*

But she kisses her daughter instead, saying only, "Good night, *querida*."

Joaquim stands up and walks Fiona to the door, watching her go, as always, as if the lingering of his gaze were enough to protect her, to keep her safe until the next time she comes home. Walking up the stairs his knees crack, making the sounds of tiny electrical shocks that have become part of the house noises, like the crackling of heaters on the first cold day of autumn.

Fiona knows that her father will probably go to bed now, rather than back to the den. And she is glad not to have stayed long enough to hear her mother step into the kitchen and unload the dishwasher, alone in the quiet house, as she has for the past twenty years, while everyone else either sleeps or waits.

In the days following her mother's anger, Leninha sulked throughout the house, dragging herself along the corridors while her mother sewed in the parlour, immobile except for her fingers. She could hear Nuno's voice in the stairwell sometimes, on his return from school, and often the sound of Sem's heavy footsteps, plodding up and down the stairs.

She had only been this unhappy once before, on a day when Vita, a girl who had cared for her longer than she could remember, had rocked her in her arms and said, "When I have my daughter I will name her Leninha, too; that way you will always be my little duck, all right?"

Leninha hadn't understood, and was confused by the tenderness with which her mother had dressed her the following morning, after Vita had gone.

"You're a big girl now, Leninha," her mother had said.

It was Branca who took pity on her this time, after watching Leninha pick at her lunch, alone in the kitchen, for what seemed like an eternity. The girl's mother had left earlier in the morning for an unnamed place, without mentioning when she would return. Branca understood from this that her mistress would be gone for most of the day.

"I believe your mother will be away for a few hours, Leninha. I don't think anyone would notice if you went downstairs."

Leninha had tiptoed into Nuno's house clutching the hem of her dress. When he looked up from his train his smile was so big she thought that it would jump off his face and swallow her whole.

Leninha and Nuno played together, from that day, in short bursts of time and always in secret. After a while, Leninha stopped hearing the sound of Sem's footsteps on the stairs, and learned from listening to her mother and aunt talk that the Professor had gone to teach in another country. The family that replaced Sem's had no young children in it, and Leninha would not have known them if it had, because she, too, was sent to another country of sorts, a convent school for girls where her mother placed her after she turned ten and her father died. Here Leninha missed Nuno very much, but soon learned to love other girls with a passion she had reserved only for him, and a teacher who always pulled back a lock of hair from her forehead, saying, "Daughter of God."

At sixteen Leninha thought she loved God as much as she could love anyone, until she bumped into Nuno again, at a corner café where her mother had once bought her a *Pirolito*, her favourite drink. Leninha loved this drink because its cap was made with a glass marble that you had to pop into the bottle with your thumb before tasting the liquid inside.

"You're back," Nuno said.

"You're so tall," she said.

He laughed, and it was then she recognized his face again. Later that week he met with her in the church of Santa Clara, on an afternoon when it was empty, and kissed her behind a column, his lips trembling and his damp hands on her breasts. She thought that she had killed him, for a moment, when his body convulsed and he leaned against her, spent, as though she had taken his last breath and used it for her own survival.

Leninha turns and turns the earth. She doesn't know what the bed will contain yet, only that she must prepare it, dig her hands in, make it rich. She is all alone, in a far corner of the garden, between the two tall trellis walls that make up the back room. For a garden has to have walls if it is to enclose, protect. And Leninha's is a garden of many rooms, created over the years from an ordinary suburban lot, a green carpet of grass laid over three inches of soil, and beneath, a layer of white gravel. She has spent years digging up that crushed stone, replacing it painstakingly with real earth, manure, rotted leaves. No one would recognize it now, the blank rectangle that she has transformed into a garden where her husband and children come to rest. Leninha seldom rests here, preferring the crushing of earth between her palms, the pulling of weeds, or the hour before break-fast, her favourite time, when she walks through the wet air with a pair of scissors in her hand.

She thinks she may plant a few calla lilies here, among the hostas. Most of her white flowers fill this back room, where the New Dawn roses climb the arbour entwined with white clematis, *jackmanii, alba*. Leninha has learned this second language of gardeners quite easily, summoning up vestiges of Latin from her days at the convent. She even encouraged her daughters to take it in school, almost nostalgically.

"Latin is a dead language, Mom," they said.

You wouldn't think it, staring at the plants in Leninha's garden that seem to grow out of their names almost audibly. Artemisia, campanula, astilbe, sedum. Words like silent caresses on her tongue.

In the very centre of the garden, a round room enclosed in boxwood, Leninha has planted a peony tree, *paeonia*, whose flowers are twice the size of her outstretched hand. Closed, they are the shape of lemons, dark pink, their centre yellow as an egg yolk. Around this tree she has planted hundreds of tulips in all colours. From the second floor of the house this bright circle of colour looks almost artificial, like the bottom of a jar filled with jelly beans, a mandala from which bits of colour have been stolen in order to populate the serious, calculated borders elsewhere in the garden.

"This is where you went nuts, isn't it, Mom?" her daughters tell her, laughing.

Leninha often stares at the mass of tulips, among them

a handful of Black Parrots given to her long ago by a man she loved. Staring at her garden, over the years, Leninha has often imagined that all its plants were gifts from her lover, the bulbs and roots so anonymous that they would never have aroused suspicion, the way a jewel would, or a bouquet of long-stemmed roses. But of course there are only these few, petals lush as dark velvet, to remind her of a man whose face she has almost forgotten.

The garden contains other secrets as well. Butts of cigarettes that she smoked in hiding, long after she had quit. A mound of river pebbles that she stole from the fountain of a plush hotel where she and Joaquim stayed. She has even buried her daughters' baby teeth at the base of the magnolia tree, on a day when she had dug until her hands bled, as if in digging she could also bury the thoughts that would invade her brain, images of smashing small heads, dropping babies from high places. The teeth have rested there, precious as the green glass marble she had saved from a broken *Pirolito* bottle and kept at the bottom of a drawer, without her mother's consent.

No one knows what a monument to Leninha's anger this garden is. Walking along the pebbled paths, the lavender borders, pausing to smell the lilies by the pond, they all ask her, amid the praise, "Where do you find the time?"

"Well," she laughs, "I have no pets."

But Joaquim, who has watched his wife bent over some plant at the oddest times of day or even in darkness, and often in her nightgown, who has seen the reddened knees marked with branches and grains of stone, knows that it is the garden that keeps her here, and sane. Looking up, she sometimes sees his shape at the window, staring at her. Leninha lifts up her hands, then, blackened with earth, and smiles at him with utter love, restored, as though the whole garden were an offering, given to him in penitence and gratitude.

Her mother and her aunt sit, side by side, on the sofa in front of her.

"Sit down, Leninha."

It is her aunt who speaks first: "We know that this is difficult to understand, but when you are older you will be thankful that it was so."

Leninha knows what is coming.

"You are not to spend any more time with Nuno," her mother says.

"Why not?"

"He isn't the right boy for you, Maria Helena. You aren't children anymore——"

"Exactly. I'm not a child anymore, Mother."

"But you obviously don't know what is best for you," her aunt says.

Leninha wants to ask her aunt where her husband and son are, knowing that this question could wound her, like a knife. Instead she says, looking only at her mother, "Please. I like him, I want to be with him."

Helena looks pensive, tired, far away, as her daughter has so often seen her, unreachable, even with words. It is this face Leninha so often tried to waken, throughout her childhood, as on the day when, aged three, she asked her mother if she could throw the turtle. Yes, yes, her mother had said, dismissing her, discovering only later that the turtle had been thrown from the balcony and splattered all over the back terrace.

It is Magdalena who brings her mother back to reality, this time.

"Don't give in," she says. "Don't let her make the same mistake."

Leninha thinks that if she smashed a turtle at their feet right now, they wouldn't flinch. Looking at her mother and aunt she wonders which of the two women she hates more.

The old ladies can't shut up. Leninha bends over the table, pulling hamburgers out of bags, dropping fries onto plates.

"What's this?" asks Magdalena.

"Ketchup. You dip the potatoes in it."

"Ah."

"Is there any water?"

"I'll get it in a minute, Mother."

"Of course, there must be one back home, we just haven't gone to it yet."

"What wonderful potatoes."

"They don't, Auntie. There isn't a McDonald's in Lisbon."

"What's this?"

"Ketchup, Mother. Didn't you hear me?"

"You dip the potatoes in it," says Magdalena.

Fiona walks into the fray. Notices her mother's troubled face.

"Oh, *querida*, how are you?"

"You look exhausted, Mom," she says.

Leninha straightens her back. "I'm all right," she says.

Helena unfolds a hamburger close to her eyes and peels off three slices of pickle, letting them drop onto her plate.

"What are those?" asks Magdalena.

Leninha disappears suddenly, while Fiona gets the drinks. She pours out the juice and settles the old ladies.

"Where did Leninha go?" they ask.

Fiona finds her mother digging in the garden, her face red and blotchy, crying like a girl.

"I can't take it anymore," Leninha says.

"They'll only be here a few more days, Mom. You have to relax."

"How can I relax? You see how they are. I could scream and they wouldn't hear me."

"They're old, Mom."

Speak up, dear, we can hardly hear you. Speak louder, Maria Helena. We can't hear you.

"I used to think she would love me more if I spoke less, if I didn't speak at all —— She was so silent. By the time I got to the convent my voice was so small, no one could hear me ——"

"Come on, Mom," says Fiona. More than anything she cannot bear this, her mother's liquid eyes, imploring her.

"You're very much like her, you know. I so often think of you, when I read her letters, you sound so much alike, did you know that? So full of kindness and wisdom.... And in person you are both a little bit cold, you keep a distance. You even walk like her."

"Mommy ——"

"You don't understand, Fiona. There is nothing that I can give them. Nothing."

Leninha stands up and brushes the dirt from her knees. "I'm going for a drive," she says. "Tell them I went to the store, or something."

Fiona sits back among the flowers, recalling other moments like this, when she has failed to rescue her mother. She has a sudden vision of Leninha bent over the kitchen counter, sobbing, with Joaquim standing helplessly beside her, saying only, "Come on, Lena, come on...."

"I've never been so unhappy in my life," her mother had said.

Fiona must have been five or six, then. She remembers now, crouching to the floor and gathering up the pieces of a plate that someone had smashed, holding them in her small hands as if in doing so she could restore her mother's joy.

Fiona wipes the earth from Leninha's garden tools and sets them on the grass. After a time, she gets up and walks back into the house, carrying with her all the unarticulated love that her mother has craved, like an uncomfortable skin she is unable to shed.

Of course, Leninha has seen him at other times, throughout her life: The man in the coffee shop who had sat next to her, smelling of old sweat, and lit a half-smoked cigarette. A young girl had walked over to him and said haughtily, "*C'est la section des non-fumeurs ici.*" She could do nothing more than shuffle off, irritated, after his astonished reply: "Well, we learn something new every day, don't we?"

Or the man she had seen walking along St-Lawrence

Street, stark naked, on a day in November, his skin red from the cold, his penis flapping under a bloated belly, his whole body bouncing along the street gleefully. "Poor man," Joaquim had said. How sad, they would all have said, staring at the homeless faces, the drunks, the bag ladies searching shamelessly through trash cans. But what strikes Leninha about them is how free they are. Freer, all of them, than she has been for a single day of her life.

She sees him again, now, standing on a corner, a grey-haired man with Sem's face. She stops the car and gestures towards him to cross, as if to tell him that he is safe, that while she waits in her car, behind the glass, no harm will come to him. She wants him to feel honoured, blessed, important.

He pauses for a moment, surprised, and then he smiles at her with a face of such beauty and grace that it fills her with pain.

VII

QUINTA DAS LAGRIMAS

As filhas do Mondego a morte escura
Longo tempo chorando memoraram
E, por memória eterna, em fonte pura
As lágrimas choradas transformaram.
O nome lhe puzeram, que inda dura,
Dos amores de Inês, que ali passaram.
Vêde que fresca fonte rega as flores,
Que lágrimas são a água e o nome Amores.

Luis de Camões
Os Lusiadas, Canto III

The nymphs of the Mondego were long to remember,
with sobbing, that dark dispatch; and their tears became a
spring of pure water, that remembrance might be eternal. The
fountain marks the scene of her earlier happiness, and is still
known today by the name they gave it, "Inês the lover."
Lucky the flowers that are nurtured from such a source,
its name telling of love, its water of tears.

"When you go there you will see her, surrounded by angels. A small crown on her head, and her face smooth, smooth as your face looks when you are lying down, at rest. And the angels cover her body with their hands, but at the same time they seem to be telling her to rise up — It's strange — as if they were telling her to leave the tomb. Well, perhaps they know the story, too. They know that Pedro is waiting for her. *O Justiceiro*, they called him, because he was absolutely ruthless in the pursuit of justice, one of the cruellest kings we have ever known. But it all started with Inês, his great love. You know, sometimes that's how it is with the people who love the most: they are also the ones who can destroy the most.... I'm going to tell you the story, *querida*, because it is one of the most interesting tales in our history. Of course there are many and I've studied them all; as you know, history is like a hobby for me, along with my travels. Every place has its own legends, but the story of Inês de Castro and Dom Pedro is one of the most beautiful, and true, you will see.

"Inês de Castro was a noblewoman, a descendant of a great noble house in Spain, which in those days was known as Castile. And she came to the Portuguese court as a lady-in-waiting to the princess, then married to the young prince, Dom Pedro. As you know, in that epoch, marriages were arranged for reasons that had nothing to do with love, and, as luck would have it, the young prince landed with a girl who didn't attract him in the least. Who knows, she may have been very kind, or pious, but perhaps she was a little bit ugly, or had bad breath, or something. And even when we *do* choose our husband or wife, there are never any guarantees, because we seldom know who people really are, or who they will become, or who *we* will become.... In any event, the young Pedro fell desperately in love with this Spanish beauty, Inês, and whenever his wife entered a room surrounded by her ladies-in-waiting, it was Inês he could not keep his eyes off. As you can imagine, the young princess was not too thrilled by her husband's wandering eye (because a woman can always tell when her husband loves another), and Pedro resolved to stay away from the court as much as possible by going on long hunts, or campaigning on behalf of his father, King Afonso IV. But no matter where Pedro went, and even on the bloodiest battlefields, he could not forget the beautiful Inês, with her alabaster skin and her dark hair. And on his return to court one morning, he found her alone in a hall and, naturally, he could no longer resist.

"Well, she became his mistress. Pedro sent her to live in Coimbra on a beautiful estate which is known today as the Quinta das Lagrimas. No, not a farm, *querida*. *Quinta* refers to the land on which a house is built, and a beautiful house it was, surrounded by gardens, orchards and forests of pine and eucalyptus, not far from the banks of the

Mondego River. He came to see her whenever he could, if he wasn't away at battle or needed at court, and she was quite happy, but like any mistress she also suffered, because a mistress can never truly belong to the man she loves, and the agony of his absences is often unbearable.... In time she bore him three children, and these were the great joy of her life. They were a part of him that she could claim as entirely her own.

"The young princess, his wife? Interesting, but no one ever seems to ask about her. Even the historians don't mention her name. I will tell you, though, because everyone merits a name, at least. She was called Constanza, poor thing. She was one of those minor characters, you see, and she died young, in the year 1345, leaving behind a son, Fernando, who would become king after his father. An awful, wimpy fellow, totally unlike Dom Pedro, he almost let the kingdom go to ruin and fall to the Spanish. You never know, I always say, you never know how your children will turn out. It is a curious thing, how your own child can be so alien, believe me. Well.

"Now, there was another reason for which Inês was kept in Coimbra, and that was the king: Afonso IV. Afonso could not approve of his son's union with a Spanish woman, particularly a noblewoman, whose links with Spanish royalty would pose a threat to the Portuguese throne. He got word that some Spanish nobles had sent Inês to Portugal precisely to ensnare Pedro and bring him back to Spain as a potential new king, because the King of Spain, who oddly enough was also called Pedro, was such a horrible creature that they wanted to get rid of him. *He* has been known throughout history as *Pedro the Cruel*. Now, with the young princess Constanza out of the way, and for obvious political reasons, Afonso was very anxious to see his son remarry. But Pedro's passion for Inês was so great that he refused any other woman as his bride, and even after her death, they say he never took another woman to his bed. Well, that is what they say, *querida*, we'll just leave it at that. (One can never know these things for sure.) And so it was that King Afonso, both irritated with his son's obstinacy and pressured by his advisers, resolved to have Inês killed.

"It was a beautiful spring morning in the year 1355 when the three executioners hired by King Afonso dragged Inês and her children from the Quinta to the palace. Crouching at his feet, Inês begged Afonso to spare her life, not for her own sake or that of her lover, but for her children's, who stood wailing at her side. Her only crime, she said, had been to give her heart to the one man who loved her more than all the world. Afonso paused for a moment and considered sparing her life. Who wouldn't be moved, after all, by the sight of a beautiful young woman? — a girl, really, because she was only nineteen, imagine — but his fears for the throne and the anger of the people were greater than his pity, and at a nod of his head, the three assassins pulled her screaming children away and dragged her back to the Quinta, where they slit her throat.

"It was almost dark that day when Pedro returned (Afonso had chosen a day when his son had been out hunting, naturally), and he made his way into the gardens, because this was where he had so often found her, picking flowers, or sitting by the edge of a pool, waiting for his return. But what he found was her slumped shape, lying very still, her skin white as stone and the water of the pool red with all the blood that had spilled into it, the blood of his beloved Inês. It was at this moment that Pedro became *O Justiceiro*. And the sight of blood was never to move him again. He carried her limp body into the house, and later had her buried in a beautiful casket at the convent of Santa Clara, not far from the Quinta. And then he waited.

"Now you understand, *querida*, why they call it the Quinta das Lagrimas: because the earth on which she had shed so many tears of longing was also the site of her tragic death. It was our great poet Camões, whom you shall certainly read one day, who recounted how the nymphs on the banks of the Mondego cried so long that their tears became a spring of pure water, *that remembrance might be eternal*. You may want to go there and see it yourself, the place where she both loved and died. You pass through a beautiful stone arch and walk into the woods, all the while knowing that she has been here, with her lover, in this very place, and then you come upon it, a spring spilling out of the rock, cool as the earth itself. It is still called *The Fountain of Love*.

"Now Afonso, who didn't have much to look forward to except his own funeral, soon grew ill with the sickness that would kill him. (Which it did, in the year 1357.) And fearing retribution from Pedro, who was now king, the three assassins that Afonso had hired fled into Spain. Their names were Diego Lopes Pacheco, Alvaro Gonçalves and Pero Coelho. Little did they know that one of the first things Pedro would do when he came to the throne was to make a pact with his namesake, Pedro the Cruel of Spain. The pact was this: the two kings would exchange prisoners, and each would capture his men at the same appointed time, so that the taking of one group might not alert the other. The day arrived, and our Pedro's men were gathering in a town near Seville where Diego Lopes Pacheco, Alvaro Gonçalves and Pero Coelho were known to hang out. And as they waited and plotted, they paid no attention to a beggar who sat close by with his back against a tavern wall. The beggar, who looked quite dumb and tattered, was actually sharp of wits, and he understood that one of the prisoners the soldiers were talking about was a man who had often given him alms: Diego Pacheco. And so the beggar resolved to repay him the favour by giving him words of advice. He shuffled off to the edge of the town and waited for Diego behind a tree, and signalled to him when he saw him approaching. Within moments, the two men had exchanged clothes, and Diego walked away among a group of poor who were on some pilgrimage. In this way he saved his own skin, and was never seen or heard from again. As for the beggar, he returned proudly to the town wearing a nobleman's clothes, and drank himself silly with the money Diego had left him in a pocket.

"The two others, Alvaro and Pero, were not so fortunate. They were taken to Portugal and brought before Pedro who decided to kill them in the most gruesome way that he could think of: by cutting out their hearts, one from the front, and one from the back. And then, so that no one would underestimate the depth of his fury, Pedro bit into each heart in front of all who were present, the blood dripping down his chin as if he had just eaten a juicy piece of meat (which it was, in fact), or an overripe fruit. From that moment onwards, Pedro devoted himself to repaying crime with cruelty: he slit throats, had men hanged and tortured and burned women, particularly if they were found guilty of adultery. A lovely character, as you can see. But there was one more thing he would do for his lost love: make her a queen.

"The people at court thought that they had seen enough horror to last a lifetime after Pedro had had his revenge on Inês' assassins. But they were wrong. On that same day, Pedro travelled to Coimbra and had her body removed from its coffin and brought to the church of Santa Cruz, down in the centre of the town. If you go there you must see the *azulejos, querida*, they are very beautiful. It is in this church that our great King Afonso Henriques is buried; as you know he was the first successfully to expel the Moors from Portugal, by conquering Santarem and then Lisbon in 1147. (Earlier he had fought his own mother, Queen Teresa, and her lover, Fernão Peres, and had them banished from the country, but that is a whole other story. . . .) And it was here that Pedro had Inês' body removed from its casket, dressed in regal robes and placed upon a throne. He told all who were assembled there that he had secretly married Inês and that she was their rightful queen, and he ordered everyone present to pay homage to her corpse and kiss her decomposed hand. She was then returned to the casket (probably nothing more than a bunch of bones by then; she had been dead for more than five years), and carried in state to Alcobaça, where a beautiful monument was waiting for her. And all along the way, as it grew dark, the men carried torches, so that she was always surrounded by a circle of light.

"It is exquisitely beautiful, the light that falls onto her face and that of her lover. At certain hours the stone turns warm and golden, like bread. No one knows who carved the two tombs, his resting on lions, symbols of his rage and revenge and hers on strange creatures, animals with human heads. Looking at these grinning beasts, you know that they are her assassins, condemned to carry her on their backs for all eternity. It was Pedro, you see, who commissioned the monuments and ordered that they be placed on either side of the altar, their feet pointing towards each other. In this way, on the Day of Judgment, he and his queen would wake from their sleep of ages, and the first thing each would see would be the other's face. Most beautiful of all is the wheel of fortune at his feet on which are inscribed, at his request, the words: *Ate o fim do mundo.* Yes. *Until the end of the world.*

"Lovely, isn't it?

"That's how it is, *querida.*"

VIII

THE GIFT

Toronto, Canada, 1994.

The garden is beginning to take shape. This is the second day of digging; Fiona's hands are covered in blisters, unlike Leninha's, which are calloused, well-seasoned, gardener's hands. Leninha has come from Montreal to help get the garden started. They have made steady progress: the beds at the back are ready, the earth mounded, black and moist, ready for the bright-green plants that will triple in size within a season, bear flowers within a year. Fiona has insisted on a blue garden, and Leninha has chosen the plants carefully, sometimes against her own instinct. Leninha hates delphiniums. But it will be lovely, in the end; it will be Fiona's.

"Strange to have planted a tree right smack in the centre, like that, don't you think, Mom?"

Fiona places her hands on her hips and contemplates the tree that stands dead centre in her backyard, its gnarled branches forming a circular canopy.

"That tree needs some serious tending," says Leninha.

"What kind of tree is it?"

"It's a fruit tree of some kind," Leninha says. "You know, this place reminds me of a garden we had in Beira, when I was a girl. We had a tree in the centre like that; the rest was mainly a courtyard, I suppose."

"I like that, *courtyard* sounds very European. Maybe I should just pave the whole thing over."

"Over my dead body," Leninha says.

"Or at least have a fountain, with a little putti shooting water out of his mouth."

"No. Better a gargoyle, to ward off evil spirits," Leninha says.

In a corner of the garden, Beatrice and Zoe also have their hands in the dirt. Leninha has mapped out a tiny vegetable patch for each of them, and they are busy collecting stones and worms. Beatrice is the more squeamish one.

"That's gross," she says.

"Grandma says worms are good for the garden," Zoe says.

"Not if you squish them."

Fiona is bent over an overgrown bush, hacking away at a tangle of branches in order to reach the roots. Leninha watches her, the faint trickle of sweat running down the nape of Fiona's neck, the slim hands, fingernails edged in half-moons of black earth.

"With my luck, the house will be haunted," Fiona says.

"It's a beautiful house, Fiona. And it's *yours*. Do you know how many women fantasize about having a place that is only theirs? *A Room of One's Own*, remember?"

"Not the women I know."

"I've never lived alone in my entire life. None of my friends have. Eunice is so paranoid about being alone she thinks she would kill herself if João died before her."

Fiona laughs. "I guess it isn't her fantasy, then."

"Well, she's a bad example."

Beatrice walks over to her mother.

"Zoe threw a worm at me, Mommy."

"Tell her she'll have to eat one if she does it again, darling."

Beatrice stares incredulously at her grandmother and runs to the back of the garden with a giant grin on her face. Fiona turns to her mother.

"It isn't always easy, Mom. It isn't easy getting up in the morning. And it's more difficult being in Toronto, now that I'm alone."

"It wasn't easy before, was it?"

"My God, no. Do you think I should have a pond?"

"Too much shade. You can't have everything, you know."

Leninha grabs a shovel and pushes it into the ground with the heel of her foot.

"The girls are doing fine," she says. "Look how busy they are."

Fiona stops pulling for a moment and watches her two daughters, two small heads bent close together, deep in conversation.

"Zoe won't have any recollection of us as a couple," she says. "But Bea.... Sometimes I look at Bea and I think the year of our divorce was the year her childhood ended. She'll never have it again, that feeling of complete safety. And one day she's going to remember it and decide who the guilty one was."

"She would do that whether you had divorced or not, darling."

"I suppose."

"And you?"

"I don't know. I don't know if I remember what it's like to be happy. All I feel is the absence of misery...."

"That's good. No misery is quite good," Leninha says.

The two women laugh, and Fiona sits on the damp grass.

"Do you still see him?" Leninha asks.

"Sometimes. He never stays very long."

"What does he say to you?"

"We don't do a lot of talking, to tell you the truth. But when he leaves I feel as if I've actually been alive for a few hours. I don't know if I can ever shake him, that's what worries me."

"Yes. Some men obliterate everything, for a while. He won't be the only one, Fiona."

"You mean I could go through this again?"

"Magdalena used to say that lovers are like wills, the last one nullifies all the others."

"You know what I found the other day, when I was unpacking my winter stuff? Her memoirs. I stayed up all night reading them."

"Hadn't you read them before?"

"No, I'd completely forgotten, can you believe it? I was mesmerized by them. She was extraordinary."

"Yes, they're very moving." Leninha stands up and leans her back against the tree. Her hair has gone grey and her skin is translucent, a faint trace of pink under high cheekbones, blue eyes. Leninha has never looked so beautiful, Fiona thinks.

"Can you imagine what a woman like that would have accomplished, today?" Leninha says.

"What ever happened to her son?"

"No one knows. I've often thought that I would love to meet him, after all these years, and get his version of things. She wasn't an easy woman to live with, you know. She would control every breath you took if she could."

"Did you know Alberto?"

"Yes, I saw him all the time. He was a very elegant man. I liked him because he had a car, and a chauffeur, and they often took me along on rides with them. He was crazy about her."

"I wish they'd known me when I was older," Fiona says. "I mean I wish they could see me as I am now."

"They would be proud of you," Leninha says. "They never could stand him, you know."

"You mean Neil?"

"They called him *that horrible creature*."

Fiona smiles. "You never told me!"

"You wouldn't have wanted to know."

"Do you miss them?" Fiona asks.

Leninha hesitates. "No, not really. I miss their letters, though." Leninha starts digging again. "You know what the saddest moment for me was? After Magdalena died and I spent those awful weeks emptying her apartment and placing my mother in that home. . . . I came back one morning to return the key to the landlord, and on the corner of her street I passed a pile of garbage, and one of her letters was there, on the sidewalk. . . ."

"Did you pick it up?"

"No, I left it. There were so many papers in that house."

"She loved to write, didn't she?"

"Well, it's got to come out somehow," Leninha says.

"I think I'd like to go back to Portugal this summer, when Neil has the kids."

"Oh, you'd have a great time, darling. Your uncle Amândio is staying in our apartment now, he would keep you company if we weren't there."

"Mommy, Mommy, there's something in the ground! We found something, come!"

"Beatrice and Zoe are scraping at an object of some kind, deep in the soil. Fiona digs in a small trowel and lifts. In her hand is a doorknob, a round globe covered in rust, heavy as a grapefruit.

"It looks quite old," Leninha says. "Might be solid brass, from the weight of it."

"I found it," Bea says. "It was in my vegetables."

"Do you suppose it could be original? It could have been the original knob from the front door."

"I want one too, Mommy," Zoe says.

"This could be almost a hundred years old, girls."

"A hundred! That's *so* old. That's older than Grandma," Beatrice says.

"Keep it inside," Leninha says. "It can be your good-luck charm."

Fiona holds the knob in her palm, closes her fingers around it and smiles. "Yes," she says. "I think we will."

IX

MEUS QUERIDOS MORTOS

La nuit de Décembre

There is a type of song they still sing in the narrow streets of the Alfama, where you can touch your neighbour's house by stretching your arm out of a window, and it is called *fado*. The Portuguese *fado*, Magdalena will tell you, originated from African slave songs that Portuguese sailors transformed to express their own longing, the loneliness of a life at sea. They call it, this longing, *saudade*, "a kind pain that you enjoy," she says, quoting a famous poet. "The Portuguese *fado* is *saudade* put to music," she says. But the name of the song has another meaning as well: it means fate.

The first time Magdalena read Fiona's poem she immediately wrote to the girl's mother explaining the dangers of plagiarism. *Nothing can be worse than dishonesty*, she wrote. *Leninha, you must not let her get away with it*. It was only when Leninha wrote back assuring her of the poem's authenticity that Magdalena read it again, marvelling at the smooth roundness of its words, the dancing rhymes. She wrote another letter: *Fiona*, querida. *You have the gift. Don't ever let it go to waste*. She would not apologize, but signed the bottom of the page, *Kisses and saudade from your devoted aunt, Magdalena*.

It has been years since Magdalena has read a poem

aloud, but she does this one justice, holding the white sheet up to the light, awing the ladies in the parlour of the Nau, a second-class hotel where she spends summers with her sister and dozens of other old ladies.

"Well done," say the ladies.

"Lovely," they say, "yes indeed."

Dona Armelinda, who is always a little bit behind, asks, "Who is it?"

"Dona Magdalena's grandniece, Fiona. She is only thirteen."

"Is she visiting?"

"No. She wrote the poem. From Canada."

"Oh, the poem."

Poems. Magdalena could recite so many of them still, as she did years ago for the poetry club, evenings when she and her friends read aloud and challenged each other to guess the authors. It was always Magdalena who read the French greats, Lamartine, Hugo, de Musset.

> *A l'âge où l'on croit à l'amour,*
> *J'étais seul dans ma chambre un jour,*
> *Pleurant ma première misère.*
> *Au coin du feu vint s'asseoir*
> *Un étranger vêtu de noir,*
> *Qui me ressemblait comme un frère.*

The audience, in those days, included men also. Brothers, cousins, some of them simply acquaintances of good repute. Rosario Mello, whose cologne invaded the room and who always insisted on sitting by a lamp. Maria Theresa, whose brother Mario was sometimes absent, causing her great sorrow and eclipsing any other topic of conversation. Rosalina, a fat girl with a beatific smile who exclaimed, "How beautiful!" so often that the others had to shush her. And, of course, Manuel, a man who had loved Madgdalena since before her ill-fated marriage, and had stood weeping behind a column in church on her wedding day.

Magdalena had made the mistake of inviting Alberto to one of the gatherings, on a night when he normally taught at the law faculty. He had saluted everyone sternly and then sat motionless throughout the evening, even when she herself had read those beautiful words.

> *Qui donc es-tu, visiteur solitaire,*
> *Hôte assidu de mes douleurs?*
> *Qu'as-tu donc fait pour me suivre sur terre?*
> *Qui donc es-tu, qui donc es-tu, mon frère,*
> *Qui n'apparais qu'au jour des pleurs?*

When everyone had left, Alberto had smashed a brandy glass against the floor and placed his head in his hands.

"I beg you, Magdalena, don't ever do this to me again," he had said.

That had been the end of the poetry club.

Rosalina mourned the loss of her friend: "But you were the best one," she said. "Who will read the French poems now?"

But Magdalena understood that some sacrifices had to be made, and this one would be no greater than others she had endured: lost friends, missed social occasions, an absent wedding ring. Worst of all, the three children she could have had, all his, three lives and deaths that she would carry inside her body, and none more valuable than his love. Alberto's face, when he looked at her across a crowded room, the weight of his head in her arms: for this she would give up poetry, theatre, writing. It was only after Alberto's death that Magdalena would find words again, words she had been storing, quietly, like some fortune in a secret bank account. She went back to the poems that had never left her, which she now copies and gathers in a book, for her niece in another country and her grandnieces, one of whom has the gift. She writes them letters, also, and notes which she has pasted all over her house in drawers, a will, indicating her assets and warning on the same page to *Watch your step in the vault of the Banco Espirito Santo, I have tripped there more than once*. But more precious than all of these is the journal which she has begun since Alberto's death, a companion whose presence will outlast all others. She has dedicated it to Leninha.

My Dear Leninha,

I write these pages for you, you are the only one for whom they would have any meaning. Many years from now you will look back on your childhood, and the people you remember will be like those paper dolls you used to play with — do you remember them? — they will have only one face, the face you saw when you were six, twelve, twenty. But you may have learned by then that even our memories consist in little more than illusions, and illusions have a way of disappearing, like foam on the water. Believe me, I have learned this the hard way. But reading these pages you shall have no doubt about who I really was, and you shall be my judge. I will write here all the words that my soul (which is infinitely romantic) craved saying, but couldn't. Read them as you would a novel: this one was lived by your aunt.

Deep in her heart Magdalena knows that stories unfold like wings. She will teach her lessons, describe the few broken friendships that have dotted her life, or a lifelong maid, Maria da Graça, who envied her and failed to appreciate her kindness. She will even revisit the years of Leninha's youth, *the green years of ingratitude*, she calls them, when her niece's affection had suddenly turned to incomprehensible hatred. Magdalena's life is full of betrayals. She will instruct on the histories of romance, recounting the unfulfilled courtships, naming the tokens of lost loves which she has kept for posterity, an engraved pen, locks of hair tied with ribbon, poems copied with care on the backs of photographs and on the inside sleeves of books. Leninha and her daughters will read them, years from now, gazing at the elegant handwriting and the sentimental language and peering closely at pressed vine leaves left between the pages, on which Magdalena has written dates, names of places and, always, the word *saudade*.

You must understand, in my time, love was all that existed. We women had no jobs, no television. It was our pastime, really, we lived for it. There was nothing else.

She will leave it at that, and not account for years of unexpressed regret at the lost opportunities, the waste of brilliant feminine minds forced into the monotony of needle-work and tea parties. The silence of women. *Mother used to say that I could have been a teacher at the Liceu, or an actress*, she writes, *and if I hadn't married Arthur I might have believed her — I was never very good at embroidery!*

But regret is a futile emotion, and Magdalena knows this even as she expresses the unanswerable wish, that God might have sent her a different son. She will not spare any of the details, how Eduardo grew to become a gambler and a drunk, the years he spent in and out of prison, the hovels he chose to live in, where she would often bring food and clothing and money.

After years of running to his rescue, of making myself ill with worry, I finally decided that I must be less generous, or perhaps this is the wrong expression, less of an idiot. Eduardo was no different from his father, he was not evil, really, but simply a lunatic who was born to torment me. One year after my marriage, my husband decided to leave for Africa. On that day I had stayed at the window and waved goodbye to him knowing that I would never see him again. I was twenty-two. One knows very little at twenty-two. In the following months I would go to Eduardo's crib and watch him sleep. I would place my hand on his head wondering, would he be happy, would he suffer? I kept my hand there as if in doing so I could protect him from some future evil. But nothing that I could have done would have saved you, Eduardo, your spirit left me so early....I didn't know then that I would one day have to make you disappear from my life as completely as your father had. But I don't believe in fate, my darling, I believe in will.

And here Magdalena will confess the awful secret, how she had opened the door to Eduardo's room in a boarding-house one December morning, and found him naked on a mattress, crouched over the body of another man. This is the last memory Magdalena has of her son.

Eduardo, my son, the miserable wretch whose life caused me so much anguish. On that morning I finally had to face it, that my

own son hated me as if I had been the cause of all his misery. You
will learn the lesson, too, querida, *and none is more difficult to*
bear, that our children grow up to be strangers. But there are no dra-
mas in life, we are the ones who construct dramas in our imagina-
tions. From this house all the ones that I loved have left, and only I
remain. I am convinced that we only live until a certain point, after
which we are merely vegetating, watching the ones who are still liv-
ing, who still have stories to tell. It is a little like sitting before a
great banquet and being allowed only to gather the crumbs that fall
from the table.

I am not bitter, though; in spite of the sorrows I have described
in these pages, I consider myself lucky. I loved and was loved, you see,
in a way that few people are privileged to experience in a lifetime.
I could go back and recount those early days, how we met, the con-
versations we had, try to pinpoint exactly the moment when our love
began, but one never knows how love begins, just as one never knows
why it ends. I was twenty-five when I met Alberto, and fifty when he
died. I've often thought that I am happy not to have witnessed his
old age, that his illness, in the end, was mercifully short. I remem-
ber a day we spent in Guincho, how I had asked him to drive us
there. It was our last outing. I remember how windy it was and the
pain in his face, my darling Alberto, how sad I was for you. At the
beach, you stayed in the car while I walked about for a while, before
going back. My darling, how I still suffer remembering this....

She will revisit them, all the same, the final weeks of
Alberto's life, when she could not go to him, how she cir-
cled his house, looking up at the windows, not daring a
knock at the door. The telegram that arrived one morning
in February, sent by his son, announcing her lover's death.
She will remember it, yes, the bunch of red roses that would

rest on his body, at her request, during a funeral from which she was excluded. Remember it, her walk to the cemetery on the day following, his name inscribed on the door to a monument she could not enter.

Time will dull our misery, Leninha, but nothing ever erases that kind of longing.

But there is one consolation that comes with age, she writes. *A funny thing happens, as the years pass; it seems as if the spirits of the dead get closer, that you walk with them, in the mornings, on your way to buy bread, or in the evenings, when you turn down the sheets. I think of you now so much more than I did before, Alberto, Mamã....I feel so close to you, now that I'm alone....*

But clearly, Magdalena is not alone. The stories are her companion, the histories, the letters, the poems from a grandniece filled already with the same longing, a *fado* on the page almost as beautiful as that poem, her favourite, whose last line she can never forget:

Ami, je suis la Solitude.

And she will transcribe it not only for the living, but also for the dead, mother, father, lover, friends, son. *Meus queridos mortos*, she calls them: My darling dead ones.

X

DANCE

Moments in Love

Toronto, Canada, 1995.

On the day her lover left her, Fiona's tears slid down her face in torrents, in waves, as though her whole body had been shut off save for this, a sudden flood of clear water. More than anything she would have liked it to last past Christmas, she would have made love to him in a house she would call her own, by the lights of her Christmas tree, which were red and green and blue, not monochrome, as her husband had liked them.

The Christmas tree has come and gone now, and with it Fiona's tears. Her lover hasn't come back. For a long time she had believed he would return; something in the ordinariness with which he left made her think that he would. A quick kiss at the door, familiar, as if he would come back that evening in time for dinner. They had never had a dinner, really, even though that is how he had asked her, that first time: "Will you have dinner with me?" She had never watched him sleep, or danced with him.

The tears come less often now. She thinks of him still, of course, with a learned detachment. She has hardened herself to the point of comfortability. She can have many lovers, being beautiful, as her grandmother was. Many people tell her this, how beautiful she is, strangers tell her, in coffee shops and in stores, and she feels momentarily victorious, savouring the possibilities. She has engendered obsessions of her own.

Fiona opens the door to her house and takes off her shoes. She doesn't draw the curtains or open the windows, and the house is cool and dry from having been closed all day. Half light. Her feet are tired and the house is incredibly silent. She pours herself a glass of water and puts a CD on, *The Art of Noise* it is called, a favourite of her husband's which she has managed to keep. She stands in the living-room in front of a mirror which is old and gilded, a wedding present from her parents, almost ten years ago. Her lover left no gifts in her house, even when he could have, only a pencil he had worn behind his ear one morning and forgotten, which she keeps in her bedroom, on a windowsill. She drinks the water, standing there in front of the mirror, because her throat is dry and her body dusty, as if she has been inhaling the dust of fallen leaves, pieces of leaves, though it is not yet autumn. The music begins slowly, and Fiona's body starts to sway; her eyes close. She is thinking of her lover and the young woman he has befriended, a thin-lipped nanny with flat hair who has begun to dress differently. Fiona had seen her pushing a stroller towards his house in the rain one day, a grin of pure happiness on her face. Well. She had watched him lower his eyes at other women many times before.

I hope this is easy for you——

She is no longer in front of the mirror now but in the centre of the room, pulling off her clothes as she dances faster, in time to the music. No one is watching her, not even her daughters, the little girls with whom she usually dances, as she runs her hands over her body, rocks her hips, crushes her own breasts, which are small enough to hold in one palm, and lighter now than they had been before she gave birth. She holds her nipples for a moment, softly, as her lover used to do, between a thumb and forefinger. She remembers this gesture from the last time also, when he held an empty space between his fingers saying, "I can only give you this much. There's never going to be any more."

"Do you think that's what I'm holding out for?" she'd said. "I've been loved before, you know. I know the difference."

She had rarely sounded so intelligent in his presence. Normally, she could barely speak a coherent language.

Fiona's hands slide down now, beneath her breasts, where she is wet from sweat, a trickle of water running down her belly like that awful line of dark hair that had travelled upwards, in pregnancy. Her belly button had been the colour of bone, then, strange and deformed. She is all soft and loose, now, her deflated belly has grown pale again, bearing only the faint rippled marks. Shiny, like old burns.

I hope this is easy for you, because it is killing me.

She continues the dance even though she is exhausted by now, having fed and dressed her children and worked all day. A weakness she could have given into earlier, when a pot-bellied stranger had noticed her leaning against a subway wall and said, "You look tired. Go home and rest." But she places her hands on her hips where the bones still jut out, and holds them there, like an old fisherwoman. She feels them gyrate as if they didn't belong to her, as if she no longer owned her own body, as if she were wearing red shoes . . . .

Do you think perhaps that you love me?

I think you do love me.

She had ventured this on a day when they had made love during her period. "Do you mind?" she had asked. "Some men are squeamish." He had placed his hands on her face, then, and covered her with his body as she lay bloody beneath him, and he had called her by name. His kindness surprised her and she felt grateful. Afterwards she had stood dripping blood and semen on the pale bedroom carpet, the blood and semen of a child they could have made, though this wouldn't have occurred to him.

"Hey!" he said.

"It's all right," she said. "I don't die from it, usually."

It was then she had asked him, out loud, "Do you think you love me?", and he had jumped at the question as if she'd slapped him.

Down, now, the music comes faster and louder as she cups her own ass, enters herself from behind, as her lover liked to do. She holds herself there, in the centre, where the deep joy was, filling the space his cock had occupied, dancing all the unsaid words. And the music is still playing, in the silent house, still playing as Fiona dances and spins, cries, exhales, gasps, falls, hunched over her own sex.

This is a dance of love.

XI

SONG
Gosto de Ti

Montreal, Canada, 1995.

Leninha sits at the kitchen table with her two daughters, unwrapping packages that have come from another country. It is Christmas, and the house is all aglitter with decorations, gilded garlands and papier-mâché boys and girls, some of them winged, dressed as though they belonged in nineteenth-century England, their mouths shaped like small, hollow Os: carollers. The packages, though, are not from England but from Portugal; they sound lovely even simply being held, white tissue paper crackling under the coarser, brown exterior, soft, like the onion-skin sheets her mother used to write letters on, so thin and transparent it was almost a wonder they made it across the Atlantic. It has been more than a year since those letters have stopped coming, and the pattern of their arrival, which had been unbroken for almost three decades, had grown erratic towards the end. Leninha has kept very few of those letters, not being sentimental. But she misses the voice they contained, which was more tender on the page than in the flesh.

Laura and Fiona, Leninha's daughters, know that these parcels will not hold anything too exciting, but they enjoy them nonetheless, pulling on the white strings and wrapping them around their fingers like homemade jewellery. Some of the trinkets sent will probably end up in boxes or in their own daughters' drawers: silver chains, doilies, miniature teacups played with once or twice and then forgotten. Fiona has come with her two daughters to spend Christmas in Montreal, and Bea and Zoe haven't yet expended the pent-up energy of a long drive. They dance in and out of the kitchen carrying between them a batterried puppy dog who, at the touch of a button, barks repeatedly and nudges himself forward until his hind legs pop and send him flipping through the air. Laura's daughter is still unborn but already present in her mother's body, which has grown full and round. Everyone comments on how wonderful Laura looks — *glowing* and *rosy* are some of the words they use — and Fiona and Leninha nod.

"Perhaps having a child will make her *softer*," Leninha says. Her tone is hopeful.

Still, Laura maintains that motherhood will not transform her, that her life will be basically unchanged. "Children will adapt to their parents' schedule," she says.

Fiona smiles at this with the arrogance of someone who has been there and knows better, but holds her tongue as Leninha nudges her foot under the table. Still, she is thrilled with her sister's pregnancy, thinking that perhaps they will now have something in common, something to talk about. She has no doubt that Laura's child will be a daughter, though she is unprepared for the rush of love she will feel at the sight of her niece, a golden-haired little girl whose face will speak back to her of her own childhood, Laura's face, as she knew it when they were both small and dressed in the same clothes, handmade jumpers and coats of pure wool, also from Portugal. Fiona will pull out the old photo albums, looking for resemblances, and she will recall, staring, how happy she was then.

There are other women in the kitchen as well. Celeste, married to Joaquim's nephew, Carlos, is, along with her husband, the only relative also to have moved to Canada, several years after Leninha and Joaquim. Celeste is a quiet woman who only enters the conversation when it is spoken in Portuguese, having never learned English. Leninha criticizes her for this and disapproves of the way Celeste lets her husband treat her. Carlos, though hard-working and loyal to his family, is prone to telling his wife to "jump" when it is time to leave or, "You can get yourself a taxi," and tapping the edge of the table with his fingers when he wants his coffee.

"This is what he does in public!" Leninha says.

"Poor thing," say the others.

Leninha shrugs her shoulders. "Maybe that's what she likes," she says. "Some women like to be abused."

"Don't be ridiculous, Mom," Laura says.

Eunice, Fiona's godmother, is also at the table, a teacup in her hand. She has been Leninha's friend for so long that she is almost like family and, like family, cannot easily be gotten rid of. Eunice is an outstanding cook and a troubled woman who never remembers birthdays. One of her favourite topics of conversation is food, and she loves to repeat recipes, enumerating each ingredient and describing each step, even if unasked. This habit drives Leninha crazy. Although a great cook in her own right, she operates more by instinct, and never forgets birthdays. Still, Leninha and Eunice share a history that goes back years to a time when, both young immigrants, they kept each other sane throughout the winter, and watched each other's children.

There had been a whole group that used to gather in the beginning, an adopted family that became almost more comfortable than the ones left behind. But throughout the years some left and moved to other cities, or returned to Portugal, something Leninha has vowed never to do, as if it were an act of utter stupidity, or worse, some kind of betrayal. She had often listened to the nostalgic longings of immigrant friends in the those days, and scoffed at them.

"Portugal is in the past," she would say. "I could never live there again." This was a sentiment that would change.

Leninha and Eunice's children have left home also, by now, and the two women still shop together, driving away boredom and loneliness throughout the winter, as before. They still complain about the season, using words like "blasted country" and "uncivilized," though they are by now hardened Canadians, having exchanged their vanity for pairs of Sorel boots and inelegant, down-filled coats. They have changed in other ways also, being older. Occasionally, Eunice will forget about recipes and lay the contents of her soul out for Leninha to examine.

"God, I didn't sleep at all last night."

"Why not?" Leninha will ask.

"I was writing a letter in my head, to the children,

explaining why I was committing suicide, because if Joaõ died before me I would kill myself. I couldn't stand to live alone."

"For heaven's sake, Eunice, of course he's going to die before you. He smokes like a chimney and weighs two hundred pounds and has high cholesterol and high blood pressure," Leninha will say.

"I know. That's why I'll have to kill myself."

"On the other hand, he'll probably outlive you precisely because he enjoys life and you are a health freak who will die from stress, so you have nothing to worry about."

"Do you think a bottle of pills would do it?" Eunice will ask.

"No," says Leninha. "You have to use the bag, otherwise they take you to the hospital and pump out your stomach and you're as good as new. And it's very embarrassing."

"Really? What bag?"

"A plastic bag, over your head, with an elastic around your neck. I read it in that book."

"How horrible," Eunice will say.

"It's the only way, honey. It's like the grace of God."

And Leninha and Eunice will laugh uproariously, laugh until the tears fill their eyes, like girls.

At other times the conversation will turn to sex, and Leninha, who is daring, will say something brash over coffee, and Eunice, who is generally very prim and prudish, will chime in with a gem of her own. If their men are present the jokes will be tamer, unless they have all had a big family meal together and are slightly giddy and careless from the wine.

"I don't know, Eunice," Leninha will say, "what are we going to do about these wilted cocks?"

"I swear, Leninha, these days it's like sticking a marshmallow in your ear!"

Laura and Fiona, if they are present, will stare openmouthed at their elders, and Joaquim, who only swears when he is back in his own country, on vacation, will shake his head and exclaim: "The children!" Everyone will laugh.

Some of the packages on the table are for Joaquim, but they will be opened by the women all the same. One box, they know, will contain yet another set of linen handkerchiefs sent to him by his mother, which he keeps, by the dozen, folded and ironed in his bedside table drawer, next to his wool socks. Joaquim is outside with the other men, battling a set of Christmas lights and the pine tree they go on, which gets bigger and more difficult to handle every Christmas. Leninha has ventured outside once or twice, wearing slippers and a shawl on her shoulders, convinced that she can direct the men to do a simple job more effectively.

"Good Lord, just pull it over the top," she says.

"Just a minute," says Joaquim, who is perched on a ladder.

"Not that way!" she says.

"Do you want to do this?" Joaquim is yelling.

Leninha goes back into the house.

Almost all the packages have been opened now. There are fewer, this year, because Leninha's mother and aunt, her only family, are both dead. Leninha's mother was not one to be too generous with gifts anyway. It was usually her aunt,

Magdalena, who would send a parcel or two, sometimes an old jewel or piece of porcelain among the trinkets. Leninha has them all now, the jewels, and she has begun offering some of them to her daughters, slowly, as her mother and aunt had done. Fiona, who is no longer married, wears her grandmother's wedding ring on her right hand. She is also the only one whose wrists are thin enough to wear her watch, one of the last pieces brought back.

"It isn't beautiful, but it was hers," Leninha had said, handing it over.

She stands up now, and brings another pot of tea to the table, along with some pastries.

"You know what was funny?" she says. "My mother never remembered the gifts that I had sent her, or given to her."

"They forget everything, once they're past a certain age," says Eunice.

"No, no. Even when she was fine. For years. She always said the gifts I gave her were from Joaquim. Isn't that stupid?"

"Strange."

"Well, absorbed by men until the end, I guess. I was never really there," she says.

Fiona stares quietly at the table and thinks back to past Christmases, birthdays, remembering that feeling of wearing a dress that someone else had chosen. It suddenly occurs to her.

"You know what, I don't think Neil ever gave me a single piece of clothing that I really liked, in ten years, can you imagine?"

"We can imagine," Laura says, but her smile is one of empathy, not sarcasm.

"Honey, I know many women my age who haven't had an orgasm from their husband in *thirty* years!" says Eunice.

"How horrible," Laura says. But the older women laugh, and begin to get up.

"You forgot this one, Mom. It has your name on it."

"You open it, darling, I have to start the potatoes."

"They're tapes, from Amândio."

Leninha takes a closer look. "Oh, the tapes," she says.

"What are they, Mom?"

"I told Amândio about these songs, the last time we were in Portugal. He said he would look for them. Old songs. Old songs from my mother's time."

"Let's play them."

"Wait."

Leninha wipes her hands on her apron and turns off the stove. Joaquim walks in and asks about dinner. "Soon," Leninha says. "Do you think you can survive?"

"I don't know," he says.

She places one of the tapes in the ghetto-blaster that sits on the kitchen counter and is used for its radio, in the mornings. A garbled noise comes on, and then the sound of a man's voice over strings and guitar, singing. A sound like an old gramophone, a radio heard through a blizzard.

Gosto de ti . . . . Gosto de ti . . . .

The words mean *I love you, I love you.*

Leninha bends and leans her hands on the counter.

"I remember this," she says. "I remember my mother, singing this song, screaming this song, with her head thrown back. I was only a little girl, I remember——"

And then she places her face in her hands and sobs, there in the kitchen, with the tape playing.

"Oh, why play them if they're gonna make you cry," Celeste says. "It's not worth it."

But the tape continues, the old, trembling voice, and Leninha cries, the potatoes can wait.

This is a moment of forgiveness.

Epilogue

THERE ARE NO BLUE FLOWERS
IN MY COUNTRY

The first time I saw her, she was heading for the water wearing only the bottom half of a bikini. From behind she almost looked like a boy: short straight hair and a strong back. She walked like a boy, but the face was entirely feminine when it turned, for a moment, looking back at the beach. It would soon be nine o'clock at night and the sun was still out, but the light was thinning and families were beginning to gather their things. I was sitting at the café and didn't think that she would notice me, staring from the safety of tables and coffee cups, old men pausing together, before finally calling an end to the day.

She walked straight into the water and swam for about twenty minutes, exhilarated, diving in and out, as if the sea belonged to her and the water weren't even cold. It was only later that I realized she was with him, a thin young man who had stumbled at the edge of the waves and rolled pathetically on the sand while she swam, far out. He had managed to stand, and after a time an old couple helped him up the small incline to a mound of beach bags. He was still trying to pull out his towel when she walked out of the sea and joined him. She brushed the sand from his body without any particular tenderness and lay beside him on her stomach. They laughed, and then they faced each other and kissed like lovers.

"You were at the beach," she says. "I see you at the café."

She is sitting at the reception desk of the Estoril Sol, where I have come to make a phone call.

"Oh, I'm sorry."

"Why?"

"I must have been staring."

"Staring?" She doesn't understand.

"Looking. I was looking too much."

"Oh. I don't mind," she says. "I am used to it. Your phone doesn't work?"

"I can't get through to TAP. I want to change my flight. I want to stay longer."

Her English is not perfect, but she pronounces each word very clearly. "You like Portugal?" she asks.

"Yes. My parents have a flat, up the street. They used to live here. I'm just visiting."

"You visit your own country," she says.

"Yes. I live in Canada. And you?"

"I live here, at the hotel. I live here for two years."

"Your English is very good."

"No, not so very."

"I'm Fiona," I say.

"Fiona. You are very elegant, like your name." She looks at me with clear eyes. "I'm Dzovig," she says.

I repeat the word, and before I have had the chance to phrase the question she answers: "Armenian. It means the blue sea."

Amândio's feet rest on a little rug. He has placed it in front
of the sofa, a cotton placemat on the lush expanse of Chi-
nese carpet that covers my parents' living-room. That and a
white towel on the back of the seat.

"I don't want it to get worn," he says.

"You're incredible."

My mother had warned me of this, his fastidiousness.
"The flat will be immaculate," she said. "He's made all kinds
of improvements."

Amândio. I have known him since childhood, my tall-
est uncle whose blue eyes were an anomaly in a family of
dark-eyed children. That and hair as tight and curly as steel
wool, the bundled kind my mother calls SOS — "Don't you
have any SOS? God, I couldn't live without them." My
mother admires efficiency.

"Everything works so well in the apartment," she said.
"The appliances are absolutely wonderful." I believe I am
meant to find it surprising that anything works well in this
country. This is a new thing.

But I have never met him as a woman, really, and he is
living in my parents' flat until the winter, in transit from a
divorce, like me. He speaks to me about love as if we had
been friends for years, and were the same age.

"I can accept that she left me," he says. "But to go
around telling everyone that we never really had anything,
that all those years were a lie, that I can't take."

"You seemed so much in love at first, even I remember
that."

"Well."

I tell him about an article I have read on the workings

of the brain, how colour is nothing more than a sensation of light being refracted through a lens, a radiation of wavelengths that get absorbed by cones in the retina.

"So?"

"Each cone contains a type of pigment; one absorbs red light, another green——"

"Yes?"

"So nothing really has a colour unless you are looking at it, and maybe that's how love is. Haven't you ever heard about the tree falling in the forest?"

"You're a smart girl," he says. "I didn't know if you had gone somewhere to eat. Shall I make some dinner?"

"I was trying to call the airline, but I couldn't get through. A girl at the hotel helped me. She had a secret number."

"Ah, the secret number. Did you change the ticket?"

"Yes. Two more days."

"Good. I have some nice little steaks," he says.

"She said I should go to Coimbra. She said I would like it there."

"You can do Coimbra in a day, if we leave early. I'll take you."

"Isn't there a church there, where they crowned Inês de Castro?"

"Who told you that?"

"Magdalena. She used to love that story."

I watch him bend over the stove, hands like my father's hands, placing a tray of frozen potatoes in the oven. He has aged, and grown a belly.

"I still have one, you know, one of the stones."

"What stones?"

"The gold stones, don't you remember?"

He smiles, recalling the summer when he told a seven-year-old niece to place the pebbles she had gathered on the beach in the oven, convincing her that if she left them there for a night they would turn to gold. He had painted each one at the kitchen table that evening, while she slept.

"That was so long ago," he says. "You don't still believe in magic, do you?"

"My husband used to be an actor," I tell her. "I used to take pictures of him. When I looked at the albums afterwards, I realized that there were hardly any pictures of me in them, of me alone. Maybe three, in ten years."

"He was good looking," she says.

"I used to pretend when I was with him. I would fantasize that my mother or father had died, that a tragedy had happened and I was in all this pain....I would dream of falling to the floor and crying out."

"You never did this in reality, you had no tragedy?"

"No, my life was perfect."

"And now?"

"Now? I no longer have those dreams. I had a lover for a while, but he only wanted me for sex."

"Well, even that is something."

We laugh.

"Was he good, your lover? Was he good in bed?"

"I never asked myself that question. I just wanted him blindly."

Dzovig and I are walking along the streets of Cascais, the Riviera of Portugal, where German students and English tourists fill the cafés. A stone wall stretches along the edge of the sea, and the beach is golden and dense below us, small fishing boats on the water. We have eaten grilled sardines and bread, sitting on the wall, feet dangling. And now an old man in a horse-drawn carriage passes us and calls out, "Ai, *meninas*!"

"And you, Dzovig?"

"I had a lover, too, not a husband. In Yerevan. Tomas. He was a student at the university. He was going to be architect. But he killed himself, with a gun in his mouth."

"Oh, I'm sorry."

"I fell to the floor," she says. "Then I left."

"You just left, like that?"

"Yes. I went to Paris, to Greece. I come here."

"What about your family?"

"My mother, she was, how do you say?...She was a slave. She talked and talked all the time, but no one listened to her. She cooked five foods, five dishes, over and over. Chicken, meat, meat another way, fried fish, fried meat. Same five dishes, over and over. My father worked, he came home, he ate. He always said to me, 'You will never have your mother's figure.' That was all he said. I had a sister. She never married."

"And Tito?"

"I meet him in Lisbon. Now we both live at the hotel. He works in the office, I do the desk, because of my English."

"What's wrong with him, Dzovig?"

"He has muscular disease, you know, like that famous scientist. People are sorry, they stare, like you. But he is good for me."

"Is he nice?"

"He is very nice. And he can't kill himself, you see. He couldn't manage the gun. I like that."

We have left the centre of the town, now, and walk along dusty roads towards the *Boca de Inferno,* where the crashing sea has carved a hole in the cliffs. I want to get a picture of the water hitting the rock. We stop on a giant, flat stone a few feet away from where the waves hit. To our left a man and his son hold fishing lines out to sea, their faces the colour of darkened leather, their hands red.

A giant wave crashes suddenly, sending a huge, white spray into the air in front of us, but I am too slow.

"I missed it, fuck."

"Wait. There will be more," she says.

"My daughters would love this."

"Beatrice and Zoe, yes?"

"Yes."

"What do you love most about them, your daughters?"

I have to think hard for a moment, before answering honestly.

"Their bodies. I love their little bodies. The way their mouths open when they sleep. When I look at their faces I find it miraculous that they exist."

"OK. Get ready. No, wait. First the deep noise, then the crash, then you press."

I listen, watching through the lens, watching the sea hit the rocks, as it has since the kings lived here.

Coimbra. We have driven through miles of road, past forests of eucalyptus and pine, towns where the food markets have been open since dawn, where widows dressed in black sell fruit and stray dogs run rampant. Amândio drives more slowly than I remember from our trips to Portugal when I was a girl. He always drove us to the beach then, five bodies crammed into a white Beetle, my mother laughing in the back seat. He seemed much more glamorous than my father, somehow, like a man who understood the wild side of things, a man who had no fear. I remember his hands, the leather gloves he wore to drive, which had round holes on the knuckles and at the finger joints.

He parks the car by the main road which runs along the Mondego River, a small bridge connecting the two sides of the city.

"I'll sit here and read for a few hours," he says. "Go do your exploring, and I'll meet you later, for lunch."

"Don't you want to come?"

"I've seen it all before. Go. I'll meet you under the arch, *Arco de Almedina*, you'll find it. There's a good little place there."

"Two o'clock?"

"See you later, beauty."

The shopping streets are very much like Lisbon's, paved in black-and-white mosaics and lined with shops, and I pass many students: Coimbra is a university town. Down in the centre they are repairing the façade of the *Igrega de Santa Cruz*: the church is draped in black cloth, as if the building itself were in mourning. *If you go there you must see the* azulejos, querida, *they are very beautiful.* The stone steps at the foot of the church are also black, from wear or dirt. They are covered in pink rose petals. I walk inside, but there is no wedding, as I had expected, no festival of any kind, only a dark interior where the blue-and-white-tiled walls shimmer as if by some inner light, depicting scenes I can barely understand. At the front of the church, near the pulpit, are the sarcophagi of Portugal's first kings: their bodies look small, almost childlike. I search around for a chair, a throne of some kind where he could have sat, or placed her. But there isn't even a plaque commemorating the spot where Pedro's courtiers came to kiss her decomposed hand: Inês de Castro, Pedro's murdered mistress. It was in this church that he had her crowned, though she had been dead for years. It is only a legend, I suppose, but who would choose to doubt that here, in this cool room, a man stared at the bones of his lost love and ordered a country to bless them?

I walk to the right of the pulpit and find a door on which is written *Cloisters of Silence*. I am surprised to find them empty, four stone corridors surrounding a fountain, two tiers of gothic arches repeating on the floor where the sun has traced their shadows. Water trickles from the fountain and the pigeons are at home here, nesting in the groined ceiling on carved flowers. My mother refuses to believe in God, in fate. "It is all coincidence," she says. "We last about two generations, if our grandchildren remember us. Then, there is nothing more."

But sitting in this courtyard I want the colour of sunlight on stone to bear testimony against her, the testimony of silent prayers and ancient love stories. I want her to hear the sound of folding wings.

I pass a lady on the way out, and ask about the petals.

"Oh, those are for the *Rainha Santa,*" she says.

"The sainted queen?"

"Isabella. You don't know her? She was married to Dom Dinis, who was a cruel king. She always wanted to help the poor, and would often go and bring them money, or food. One day she was carrying bread in her apron, like this, when the king stopped her. 'What have you got there?' he asked. 'Why, flowers, senhor,' she answered. 'I have been gathering flowers.' And when she let down her apron to show him, the bread had been transformed into roses, which tumbled to the ground at her feet. She is our patron saint."

"Thank you. I didn't know that story."

"It's not a story, *menina*; it's what happened."

"That's it? That's all you're eating?" he says.

"I'm full. It was delicious."

"Look at you. You eat like a bird."

"Do you know the *Rainha Santa*?"

"She fed the poor, something like that."

"She transformed bread into roses, to escape her husband's fury. A lady at the church told me."

"You see, even then women were lying to their husbands," he says.

"You mean even then women *had* to lie to their husbands."

"Fiona the feminist," he says.

"Have you ever been to wash the bones?" I ask him.

"What?"

"When grandmother's grave was opened, were you there?"

"She wasn't ready. If the body isn't decomposed they wait another five years. But it was Pepe who went. Why?"

"My grandmother, Helena. It's been five years. Mom wants me to go to the cemetery. I have this tablecloth she gave me, to line the little casket with. It's very pretty."

"The men will do it. You don't have to stay."

"I know. I'll take the cloth, and pay them. I'll do it on Monday, before I leave."

We leave the restaurant and walk to the car, passing tourists and women sitting on chairs who hold up signs advertising rooms to rent. One of them calls out to Amândio, "A room, senhor, a lovely room for you!"

In the car, on the drive home, my eyes grow heavy. I am still half-conscious when I feel a hand brush by my cheek and the back of my seat being lowered, slowly.

It is dark when we get home.

"You slept like a baby," he says.

"I don't know why I'm so tired. Thanks, Amândio."

I take a hot bath and lie in my parents' bed staring at the ceiling and holding myself. I don't know how much time has passed, or what I have been thinking of, when he opens the door. But walking into my room he is no longer my uncle, not even a known man, only a body who covers me with hands, and kisses like blessings. Who covers me with kindness. For there are different kinds of lovemaking; love that asks, love that needs, love that plays. But I have never had this before, love that heals. He looks at me from behind long lashes and his eyes tilt downwards, as though they were about to roll down his face. And when he enters me, finally, I feel for the first time that something has been given back, restored. He lies beside me, afterwards, running a finger along my spine, tracing the outlines of my shoulder blades.

"You have wings," he says.

"Fiona. It's me. It's Dzovig."

Six a.m. I press the buzzer to let her into the building, and open the door.

"It's six in the morning, Dzovig. Is something wrong?"

"I got Joanna to work for me this morning. We can hurry, we must get there before the tide is high. *Praia da Adraga*, you will see. I want to show you a place."

Amândio steps out of his room, confused.

"Do you have a car?"

"No." I turn to Amândio.

"All right," he says, giving me his keys.

"Do you know the way, Dzovig?"

"No," she says. "Don't worry."

We drive for about an hour, carefully, because I am untrusting of Portuguese roads, and it is still barely light out. The beach sits at the bottom of an escarpment, and giant rocks jut out of the water, as if there had been an earthquake here, hundreds of years ago, and the mountain had tumbled into the sea.

"It's beautiful," I tell her.

She takes me to the far end of the beach, around one of the outcrops. Close up the rocks are covered in tiny mussels and snails, dark green and black. My feet are freezing in the shallow water.

"Look at this," she says, and we enter a cave which

smells of wet salt and seaweed, and echoes like the inside of a shell.

"I knew you would love it, Fiona!"

"How did you find it?"

"Everyone knows it. The kids come here to pee, during the day. And lovers. But not this early. This is why I love Portugal, you know. I love the sea here."

She bends down and scoops up water in her hands, dips her tongue in, like a cat.

"In Armenia we have only mountains, not much sea. Lots of old churches, people fighting, Arabs, Turks. Many Armenians leave."

"You have to come to Canada, one day. Will you come and see me, with Tito? I've started to plant a garden. My mother is the most amazing gardener. I have roses, and globe thistles."

"Globe what?"

"Globe thistles. They are blue flowers, round, like planets, covered in tiny spikes. They're beautiful. The bees love them."

"There are no blue flowers in my country," she says. "My mother used to say, if there was enough blue in the sky to make a Dutchman's pantaloons, it would be a sunny day."

"So, you listened to her after all."

"Maybe I lied a little, it's true."

"Maybe we always listen more than we realize. I had a dream the other night. I felt a man lying next to me, and I placed my hand on him, like that. It felt so real."

"Maybe he was. Tito laughs when he dreams, sometimes."

"My daughters have done that."

The sun rises higher, and the water begins to sparkle before us.

"I miss my sister," I tell her.

"Well, you will be back soon, Fiona. What will you do when you get home?"

"I'll write."

"Stories?"

I smile. "Yes, stories."

Dzovig steps out of the cave a little and places her hands over her mouth. She begins to yell, through her hands, her tongue hitting the roof of her mouth, "La la la la la la la la!"

"Can you do it, Fiona? They do it in Iran, the women. They do it when they are sad, and also when they are happy. Come on."

I stand beside her no longer feeling the cold at my feet and raise up my arms, which are fuller now, like a woman's arms. "La la la la la la la la!" I call.

"Louder!" she says. And we both do it. We laugh and scream like women undaunted.

I have come back. I am walking the streets where my grand-mothers walked, seeking out the church where my great-aunt married. A middle-aged man helps me find it, grumbling all the way because I haven't got a name.

"How can you not know what you are looking for?" he says irritably.

Still, he takes me to a church and I know that this is the one, a white building with wide stone steps as Magdalena described it that summer, long ago, when we stayed at her house. But the square is empty, it is early in the morning and the doors are locked. I find my way to her apartment building now, hoping that I can climb the stairs and peer through the keyhole. Hoping that those rooms will still be unoccupied. The building looks different: the iron railings have been painted and the old wooden door replaced with a shiny green one, also closed. But the streets are still mine, the pavements where they have walked, holy, now, as the old eyeglasses my mother showed me, saying reverently: *what she saw the world through.*

I save my grandmother's house for last. It was the smaller of the two: a tiny apartment in a nondescript building where I seldom came as a girl. What I remember from it is my grandmother's bedroom, where the bed stood pristine and the marble-topped furniture gleamed, and another room, full of books. I know the smell of those books as clearly as I know the smell of my daughters' heads.

I have a new house to come to, now, in Portugal, a flat my parents have bought which is filled with beautiful lamps and portraits, my mother's spirit pervading every detail, waiting for the imprint of new memories. This is the house my daughters will see, years from now, in visions of themselves as little girls in another country, a country both foreign and familiar. A country my mother has now reclaimed, returned to as from a self-imposed exile.

It is ten o'clock and I must get to the cemetery. They are going to exhume my grandmother's bones, clean them and place them in a smaller casket, which will go into a vault. One must make room for the dead, in these old countries.

They are all here: Leonor, my great-grandfather; Magdalena, my grandmother. I walk between rows and rows of graves, mounds of earth outlined in white marble, covered in flowers, the crunch of pebbles beneath my feet. The flowers are everywhere, red, yellow and pink, and the place is covered in sunlight. They call it *Cemeterio dos Prazeres*: the Cemetery of Pleasures. Here and there are the mausoleums, small stone temples housing the wealthier families, the aristocrats, the politicians: the important dead. I read their inscriptions with a vague curiosity, unsure what I am looking for, and then I am trembling, suddenly, in front of a bronze door bearing a name I recognize. I run my fingers over each letter, mouthing the words as in a prayer: *Alberto Francisco Machado, Juiz do Supremo Tribunal, Lisboa, 1877–1951*.

It has been five years since I have stood here, with my mother, watching men dig. Since then she has aged, suddenly. Death resolves so little, in the end. Thinking of my children I realize that I can never duplicate in intensity the passion with which my mother loves me, that my daughters will never love me as I love them. But I am no longer embarrassed by overwhelming love. And I understand that none of my suffering is new. There is a comfort in this.

Why have I come?

I have come for fountains shaped like quatrefoils, trickling in courtyards. For the smooth stones of pavements, walked on for centuries. For the taste of sugar in my mouth, mornings on the beach. For old men in horse-drawn carriages who call me *menina* and other men, whose eyes and mouths travel up and down my body: like children, they are unashamed of their desire. I have come for kings and queens encased in tombs, and thin dogs gnawing on chicken legs in open markets and rose petals on the steps of churches. I have come for the ever-present sea and the precipices that beckon, *Look, will you choose to die today? Look how easy it is to fall off!* For the huge statue of Christ whose head bends over the city, in this country of old saints and stone.

I walk to the far end of the cemetery and give my name to an attendant. A few moments later, two men appear and I follow them into a square building. They wash my grand-mother's bones in a deep basin and set them out on a towel to dry. The air smells like wet wool.

"I've brought this cloth," I tell them.

"You can bring it into the next room, *menina*."

I line the small casket with it, leaving lengths of white linen on either side, enough to cover. One of the men walks in with a bunched-up towel, and the bones tinkle inside it as he sets it down.

"Well, now," he says.

"Please," I tell him, stretching out my hands. "Let me."